I0601105

To Alison McDonald

Group Therapy

MARGARET LYGNOS

Contents

Cast of characters

FELICITY   Social worker, married to Jack, two teenage daughters.

MANDY   Retired nurse, married to John, one adult son George and daughter Poppy.

ASTRID   Registered nurse, divorced, one young daughter Julie.

JANE   Home based business, separated from Rick, two young children Zoe and William

KATHY   Full time mother, divorced from Wayne, young children Amy, Ruth and Tommy.

GRACE   Lawyer, new partner to Wayne, baby Fin.

EVA   Practice manager, married to Martin.

MARTHA   Widow, mother of Eva, 95 years old.

MARJORIE   Retired teacher, widow, two adult daughters, aunt of Astrid

PIXIE   Married to James, affair with Rick, two young boys.

PEGGY   Mother of Wayne.

Prologue

I'm driving home. I have been in Melbourne for the day at an exhibition taking part in an update of my hairdressing skills, in particular hair extensions. I once lived in Melbourne but now I would never go back to city living again. Don't get me wrong, I love Melbourne and I love visiting and there is so much going on there, but I love the quiet semi-rural life more.

If you drive north from Melbourne you will eventually reach various small cities and even smaller townships and also some tiny villages. Sometimes so small you don't know they are villages, just an old church, a school, a pub, maybe a shop. There are miles and miles of paddocks dotted with grazing sheep and cows. There are rows and rows of green vegetables and huge groves of olive or apple trees. It's a beautiful drive home but nothing beats the feeling of driving under the bridge where the main road of my town begins. Up ahead I can see the gentle rise of the nearby mountain range covered in a thick green tangle of Australian flora which provides habitat for our wonderful native animals and birds.

I have lived here for fifteen years and through my business I have got to know many of the locals and some have become close friends and confidants. It is from talking to these clients and friends I became aware of the story I am about to relate to you.

"There is something delicious about writing the first words of a story. You never quite know where they'll take you."
— Beatrix Potter.

1

Meeting

The winter sun streamed through large floor-to-ceiling windows and flooded the modern room with warmth and light. It was a freezing cold day. Three women had discarded their winter coats and hats and sat waiting in a small circle of chairs. They didn't know each other but they smiled politely and waited patiently. One checked her phone, another stared out of the window whilst the third watched a tiny spider descending from the ceiling on a fine web. It twisted and turned, propelled by the gentle flow from the air conditioner as it fell further and further towards the grey carpet. No one else saw it. Tall gum trees surrounding the building hosted a large flock of noisy currawongs which carolled and called to each other as they moved from tree to tree. Suddenly an adjoining door was flung open and a tall woman dressed in a billowing floral garment and matching scarf tied around her wild red hair burst into the room.

"Hello ladies!" she said looking around the room before taking a seat. "Oh, I thought there would be four of you. Oh well, never mind, let's get started. I'm Felicity Sharpe and you obviously received my letter inviting you here today, and I must add I am very pleased to see you." All this was said with gushing nervousness.

She was interrupted mid-sentence as the same door opened again and a very overweight young blonde woman with an extremely pretty face peered nervously into the circle.

"Come in, come in," said Felicity. "We are just about to start."

The woman entered and sat on one of the chairs in the circle.

The redhead began again. "My name is Felicity Sharpe. I'm a social worker employed by the local council and the Greenmount Medical Centre. It's my initiative which has brought you here today for this meeting along with other newcomers to Greenmount. I am doing this because of a tragic event which occurred last year. I know that sounds weird but when I have told you the story, hopefully you will understand what I am attempting to do."

Felicity stopped and, taking a deep breath, she went on to explain about a young couple who had moved to Greenmount from interstate. They had no family in Victoria, they only had each other and the woman was about seven months pregnant when they arrived. The pregnancy went full term but sadly the baby was stillborn. Unfortunately the woman was discharged from hospital with no support and no one knew about her. Her husband went back to work and the woman was alone. She became severely depressed and sadly, committed suicide. Her poor husband found her one morning when he returned from a night shift at the local abattoir.

"I was so distressed by this preventable death that I decided I would try to meet all newcomers and make contact in an effort to prevent anything of the sort ever happening again," Felicity said.

The four women all murmured exclamations of shock and sympathy.

"How awful."

"So sad."

"Dreadful."

"Poor woman."

Felicity stood up and passed a colourful pamphlet to each of the women.

"This is just some general information about the shire provided by the council pointing out where to vote, the Medical Centre, the nearest hospital, schools and kindergartens, the library, the CFA, and where you can volunteer if you have any free time."

Felicity paused for a moment then added, "Most importantly, I must stress that if you ever need help or know anyone who needs help, please refer them to me. I am always contactable at the Medical Centre or the shire office. My phone number is in this leaflet. I am here to assist anyone with anything, I don't mean I can do everything, but I will certainly do my best to put you in touch with someone who can help if I can't."

Felicity sat down. Her face was flushed and she appeared to be a little short of breath.

"I still get upset when I talk about it," she said. "That's enough for now, let's sit down together and have a cup of tea or coffee and get to know each other a little and that way we will each know four more people in Greenmount by the end of the day."

Felicity led them to a comfortable lounge area where a delicious-looking chocolate cake, covered by a glass dome, was on a low table waiting to be eaten. The women settled back and began to chat while Felicity made the tea and coffee. When she returned she poured a cup for everyone then cut the cake and passed a plate with a huge slice to each of the women.

"I know it's usually done the other way around but I wanted to get the unpleasantness over and done with. So I think we could introduce ourselves properly now," said Felicity.

Returning her cup to the table she began. "I'm married, I have two teenagers who have left home and live in the city and I have lived here for many years. The rest I more or less told you before."

She nodded to the woman on her left, indicating that it was her turn to speak.

Mandy was a middle-aged woman of normal weight and average height. She wore black Doc Martens, jeans and a hand-knitted jumper. Her blonde hair was neatly cut at shoulder length.

"My name is Mandy." She said. "I am a retired nurse, my husband and I moved here because I have been unwell and I felt a 'tree change' would do me good, and it has. It's so quiet and peaceful and I love the open spaces and there are no noisy trams and there is less traffic on the local roads to worry about. Oh and the birds, I can't believe how beautiful they are."

"Thank you Mandy." Felicity indicated to the next woman.

Astrid was a tall slender woman with long, light-brown hair. The jeans she wore were tucked into knee-high boots and a firm fitted shirt emphasised her slim waist and hips.

"I am Astrid. I am also a nurse and I will be working part-time at the hospital in Kelvington. I have moved here to be near my older cousin Marjorie to keep an eye on her, and she will help me by looking after my daughter Julie after school and when I am working."

"Thank you," said Felicity, and smiled at the third woman. "Your turn."

Jane, dressed in high-heeled ankle-length boots, a black slimline skirt and a cream shirt, could have been a model. Her dark hair was long and beautifully layered and her dark eyes were looking down to her left hand, where she wore a large diamond ring.

"Jane is my name." She said quietly. "My husband and I have moved here to be closer to his job." That was all she said, and she looked at the woman sitting next to her, making it obvious that was all she had to say, so Felicity indicated to the fourth woman that it was her turn.

Kathy was young, probably in her early twenties. Her very pretty face was framed by long naturally blonde hair which needed a good cut. Her longish loose dress was worn over black tights and grubby white running shoes.

She blushed profusely and stuttered, "Kathy, I am Kathy." She looked down at her hands in her lap, making it obvious that she also had very little to say.

Felicity stood up and smiled at the group. "Thank you to all of you for coming. Please take seriously what I have said today, but now I have an appointment with the practice manager at our Medical Centre so I must go. However you are welcome to stay and talk here for as long as you like and please eat the cake, otherwise I will be tempted to eat more."

Felicity went to her nearby office, from where she could still see into the room where the four women were sitting. Looking at them she was pleased with herself for bringing them together. She thought they all seemed very nice women although Kathy appeared to be extremely shy. 'It will do her good to get to know some other women,' she said to herself. Two of them, Mandy and Astrid, were engaged in conversation; Felicity assumed they had their nursing background in common. The other two were listening but didn't appear to be taking part.

Felicity thought to herself that at least she had made a start and would like to keep in touch with these women herself. She was a caring person who wanted to be all things to all people but this caused her to become over burdened and overwhelmed with too much for one person to cope with. She was smart enough to realise this but she just couldn't help herself.

Felicity's phone rang to announce the expected arrival of the staff member with whom she had the appointment so she left the building and the four women stayed.

Kathy barely said a word but ate two pieces of cake. Jane was also fairly quiet but Mandy and Astrid both chatted, trying to engage the other two without much success. When they all decided to leave, Mandy and Astrid farewelled the other two and walked across the road together to a brightly painted organic fruit shop.

"They are both very quiet, do you think we were talking too much or are they both shy?" Mandy asked as she picked up bunch of bananas.

"I am not sure," replied Astrid. "Kathy is very young and seemed to be uncomfortable, I don't think she is more than mid-twenties. I feel a bit awful now. I'll ring Felicity and get their phone numbers and get in touch with them both."

"Yes," agreed Mandy, "why don't we arrange to meet again next week and have coffee together, then they will know we didn't intend to exclude them. It wouldn't be the first time I've scared off someone unintentionally!"

Mandy knew her direct manner had intimidated people in the past and she had made attempts to curb this characteristic, but it was easier said than done. "Maybe I need to apologise for talking too much."

They left the shop together both carrying a bag of fruit and a bunch of flowers.

"Okay, you do that and give me a ring. I can do most afternoons except Monday and Tuesday," Astrid said.

They took out their mobile phones, exchanged numbers, said goodbye and walked off in different directions to their parked cars.

2

Eva

Felicity met Eva, the woman she had been expecting, at the front desk and they walked across the road to a café where they ordered coffee and sat down near a window which looked over a small garden. Eva was practice manager at the Greenmount Medical Centre and had worked there for a number of years and was an excellent administrator. Still very attractive in her early sixties, she looked a good ten years younger. Her health was excellent and she kept herself very fit and trim by exercising and walking everywhere.

"Now, how can I help you, Eva," asked Felicity kindly.

"Well, you know that my mother was living with me for four years until several months ago when she had a fall and fractured her femur?"

"Yes I knew that. How is she now?"

"She's become quite frail since the fall and unfortunately she had another fall in the rehab centre and broke her wrist. Her femur has healed as well as it can but she can't put any weight on her leg and now she's in a wheelchair permanently."

"I didn't know about your mother's second fall; where is she living now?"

"She's been in rehab all this time but now she has rehabilitated as much as is possible and they are pushing me to put her in a nursing home. My mother has always hated the idea of ending up in a nursing home and I've always assured her that I would look after her so that it wouldn't be necessary."

"Are you going to care for her?"

"I have to, I promised her that I would, plus she had a difficult life and I want to see that her last years are happy and comfortable."

"So I suppose you are thinking about handing in your notice and retiring."

"Yes. I have always intended to work well past retirement age, this is why I gave up bedside nursing and began practice management, but at the same time I do want to do this last thing for my mother."

"Would you rather take whatever long-service leave is due and when that's up rethink what you are doing? asked Felicity.

"Yes I suppose I could, I hadn't thought of that... it sounds like a better idea, perhaps I'll do that."

"How old is your mother?"

"She is ninety-five."

"You think about it and let me know what you decide as soon as possible. I'll support your application for leave because it is short notice."

Felicity put her hand on Eva's arm in a gesture of support. "We will speak soon."

Felicity was aware that she had just added another job to her long list of things to do.

3

Eva and Martha

Martha had been living with her daughter Eva and her husband for a few years before she fell and fractured her femur. When she moved in with them she had been mobile and was able to have a shower with only a little help from Eva. She spent most of her days sitting in the sunny kitchen which overlooked a pretty garden. She read books and magazines, did the crosswords in the daily paper and watched television in the afternoon and evening. She didn't want to go out, preferring to stay at home where it was warm and comfortable. Neither did she have many visitors, because most of her old friends had died or were in similar situations as she was. She had lived a long and mostly difficult life as her husband had died at a young age and Martha had been left to care for her children on her own. She was a frugal woman, having lived through both the world wars and the great depression, and had learnt to get by with very little. After seeing her father and several good friends spend their last days in nursing homes she dreaded ending up in one herself. She had never directly asked Eva not to put her in a nursing home but she had made it very clear that she hated the very thought of it and Eva had assured her she would never do that.

One day Eva received a phone call from a woman whose elderly mother had been Martha's friend for years at the church they had both attended. They had not seen each other for more than five years as neither of them managed to get to church any more.

"Hello," said Sandra Wren, "you may not remember me but our mothers are old friends and I wondered if I could bring my mother to visit your mother?"

"Oh yes, I remember you and your mother, I'm sure Mum would love to see her," Eva agreed.

The two women arrived the next day for afternoon tea. Eva made some scones and a pot of tea, which she served to the two elderly women.

Although they had known each other since they were young women they had always addressed each other formally as Mrs McLean and Mrs Wren. It was not until they were in their late seventies that they broke with tradition and began calling each other by their given names. But now they must have forgotten as they reverted to greeting each other formally.

"Oh Mrs McLean, it's so good to see you after all this time," said Mrs Wren.

"Yes it's so good to see you too," said Martha. "How are you?"

"I'm as well as can be expected. How are you?" she replied.

"Not too bad, still alive, can't complain."

"It's been such a long time," said Mrs Wren.

Eva poured them another cup of tea and passed each of them another scone. Then, as they were exhausted from all the talk and all the tea and scones, they both nodded off to sleep. About ten minutes later they both woke up and looked at each other.

"Mrs McLean, it's so good to see you after all this time, how are you?"

"As well as can be expected, and how are you?" asked Martha.

"Still alive, can't complain," Mrs Wren replied.

"It's been a long time since I've seen you."

"Yes it's so good to see you too, how are you?"

"Still going strong."

That set the scene for the next two hours during which the two elderly women continued to greet each other, snooze a little, wake up and greet each other again. The two younger women, Eva and Sandra, found their mothers hilarious and decided to make it a regular arrangement for them to see each other.

At Christmas time Eva and Martha were thrilled to receive a visit from a small group of carol singers from their local Baptist church. They came to the house specially to sing to dear old Martha. She had some notoriety at the church because she was the oldest living member of the congregation. Perhaps this is why she was given this special treatment. The choir consisted mostly of children accompanied by their parents who came into the house and sang beautifully Silent Night, Away in a Manger and Oh Come All Ye Faithful. Martha was delighted to have such a personal performance from the church she had attended for over sixty years. One of the adults asked after Martha's health which was pretty good really for a woman of her age. Eva answered, "She is in very good health and I always give her a glass of wine with her dinner."

Two of the dear little Baptist children turned and stared at Eva with looks of shock and disbelief on their innocent little faces. Eva had forgotten that it was a sin to drink alcohol if you were a good Baptist; no dancing either. After the carollers left Martha said to Eva, "Did you have to tell them that?"

"Oh Mum, it's about time they opened their eyes and joined the real world. Most people like to drink wine. What if I had told them you liked to dance—you know what that leads to!"

"Not any more," said Martha.

They both had a giggle over that.

After Martha had been living with Eva for several months she went to stay with Eva's brother Allen and his wife Jacky for a month while Eva and her husband Martin went for a trip overseas. They had a great time but were really upset when they arrived home to discover that Allen and Jacky had booked Martha into a nursing home without consulting anyone else in the family.

Eva had rung her brother to say they would pick Martha up on Friday as the jet lag should have passed by then, and was told "you might as well leave her here because she is going into a nursing home near us next Monday."

"What!" exclaimed Eva. "Who decided that?"

"Jacky thought it would be better for all of us because she has found it very difficult to care for her while you have been away," Allen replied.

"What does Mum think about that?" Eva asked.

"We haven't told her yet."

"Oh come on, that's not very nice. I don't agree with that." Eva slammed down the phone.

Eva went immediately to Martin to tell him. He was very annoyed that they had made that decision without asking them or in particular not asking Martha.

"We had better go and get her," he said.

Poor old Martha was confused about where she was and what was happening to her. Although Eva had told her they would be back and would take her home with them after their holiday, she had forgotten. When she saw Eva she cried and said, "I didn't think you wanted me any more."

"Oh Mum, of course I want you, and I am taking you home right now."

As they drove home Martha said, "please don't send me there again."

"No I certainly won't," Eva assured her, and she meant it. The older she got the more she felt sorry for Martha and the more she understood her, even though they were so different.

Unfortunately Martha fell one day trying to walk to the toilet without her walking frame. Eva found her on the floor struggling to get up and she was in a lot of pain and very confused. Her femur was fractured and during the difficult repair that night she almost died. After discharge from hospital she was admitted to a nearby rehabilitation hospital where she spent the next six months.

4

#

A week after the meeting with Felicity Sharpe, Mandy and Astrid walked into the local café at the same time and found Jane and Kathy already at a table waiting for them. Coffee and cake were ordered and Mandy tried to get Kathy to open up a little but it was hard work. Kathy blushed often and it was obvious she lacked self-confidence. Secretly she was surprised that these women would want to know anything about her.

"Do you have children, Kathy?" asked Mandy.

"Yes I have three."

"School age?"

"Two at school and one at home."

"Is that child at kindergarten?"

"No, he doesn't go to kinder yet."

"Is he at home with his dad?"

"Oh no." She looked at her watch and stood up to go. "I have to go, goodbye."

Kathy hurried out of the door.

Mandy was shocked, "Well I blew that didn't I?"

"Never mind, she is just very shy," said Jane.

"Yes but I think I upset her and that wasn't my intention. Sometimes my direct manner is a bit intimidating."

It was decided to look out for Kathy at drop-off or pick-up at school and invite her to the next time they were meeting for coffee. But neither Astrid nor Jane saw her at the school and they did not know who her children were to ask about their mother. But they didn't forget about her.

5

Kathy

The first time the women met at the café, Kathy had left abruptly, hating herself for doing so and knowing the other women would think it an odd thing to do, but she had to; she was ashamed and embarrassed and could not tell them about herself. She liked being with them even though they were all much older than she was. She could hardly believe these mature, well-dressed women wanted to include her in their gatherings.

Why couldn't they just let me sit and listen to them talking and let me feel like I am one of them? she thought to herself. Wasn't it enough that I was there and not at home sitting on the couch, eating, watching TV or, even worse, still lying in bed?

She liked the women and they had exchanged phone numbers with her. She wanted to be like them and she wanted them to like her, but now she had ruined any chance of that happening by running out of the café like a frightened animal. She had paid attention to what they did and what they ordered and she had done the same. They had skinny cappuccino so she had a skinny cappuccino but then she spoilt that by putting three spoons of sugar in her cup. Mandy had noticed, she just knew she had, and she had tried to pretend it was a mistake and had made herself look even sillier. She hurried home and consoled herself by getting stuck into a two-litre tub of choc-chip ice-cream. Afterwards she felt even worse and made herself vomit in the bathroom. As she stood up from the toilet bowl she caught a glimpse of herself in the mirror, her eyes red and watering, her hair stuck to her blotchy face. She hated what she saw. She began to sob and berated herself for her lack of self control and terrible eating habits. Kathy was trapped in a vicious cycle and the result was despair and self-loathing.

Kathy had twin girls, Ruth and Amy, who were seven years old. They liked school and walked to school alone most mornings after getting their own breakfast and making a jam sandwich each for their lunch. Their teacher had noticed they never had fruit or anything other than a jam sandwich and wondered if she should speak to their mother about it, but she never saw their mother to bring up the subject. She asked the girls to tell their mother she wished to meet her but she did not get a response.

Kathy felt dreadful that she was forcing her two little girls to do so much for themselves but some mornings she just couldn't get out of bed. And then there was her third child, Tommy, who was just three years old and not very well. He was a small, pale boy with grey eyes and a smattering of freckles across his nose. He never looked happy and cried at the slightest thing which annoyed Kathy. He suffered with asthma and this winter had been hospitalised several times because he had had difficulty breathing and his puffer just didn't seem to help. Each time he had responded well to treatment in hospital and was discharged promptly. Each time a nurse had gone over the correct way to administer the Ventolin via the plastic spacer, thinking that Kathy was not using the proper technique.

Kathy felt awful about this also because she knew very well how to administer the Ventolin, she just had not done it at all. She knew it was wrong but she had her reasons. When Tommy was admitted to hospital, Wayne, her ex-husband, would rush in to see him and that meant she got to see Wayne. She still loved Wayne and she missed him so much it hurt, and the thought of her tall handsome Wayne with that other woman hurt even more; in fact it was really driving her crazy.

Wayne was a plumber running his own business. He had plenty of work and sometimes worked seven days a week. For this reason Kathy had not been suspicious when he became involved with Grace. Wayne had done some work for Grace who was updating an old house. It had been more complicated than first thought so he spent three weeks at Grace's place under the house, on the roof, in her new bathroom, under the kitchen sink and in the garden installing a huge stainless steel gas barbecue under the new pergola. During this time they got to know each other over coffee in the afternoon or a glass of wine at the end of the day. Wayne knew he should get the job over and done with quickly and get back to being a faithful husband to his childhood sweetheart Kathy but he was not being ruled by his head. Wayne and Grace talked and laughed about so many things and through this he realised how much he was missing in his relationship with Kathy, where they rarely spoke about anything of interest or importance.

Kathy and he had known each other since they were teenagers and both still at school, and had married when she turned eighteen. He was tall and good-looking and she had been a petite, pretty, blue-eyed blonde. Kathy had given birth to the twins early in the marriage and never lost the baby weight, and then with Tommy she put on even more weight. Wayne's mother and sisters had encouraged her to breastfeed saying it would help her to lose the excess weight. But she said she just could not imagine having a baby sucking at her breasts. Being overweight made Kathy depressed and self-conscious so she used food to make herself feel better and then felt even worse after overeating. Wayne had tried to help her but nothing he said or did helped her to regain her self-confidence. Wayne had paid for weight loss meals for several months but Kathy didn't lose any weight because she still ate Danish pastries, chocolate and ice-cream every day. When Wayne found out he cancelled the meals without telling her so when the meals did not arrive, Kathy knew Wayne was aware of her lack of self-control. The more Kathy disliked herself the more distant she became, and the thought of Wayne seeing her naked or even feeling her fat body filled her with dread. So there was no sex between them any more. Kathy slept most nights with one of the children and Wayne began to feel unappreciated and unloved—after all, he reasoned, he was providing for his family, working very long hours, earning quite a bit of money, so surely he deserved a little bit of attention from his wife. He never forced himself on Kathy and because of the problems in his marriage he was more than happy to be away from home working long hours.

The plumbing work at Grace's house finished on a Thursday night and Grace surprised Wayne by inviting him in to her dining room for a meal to celebrate.

"I can't sit at that table like this," said Wayne. "I am dirty."

"You can have a shower in my beautiful new bathroom if you like."

"Okay, I will. I've got an old pair of jeans and a shirt in the car, old but clean; I'll put them on."

Wayne entered the dining room where Grace had the table set for dinner in the newly decorated room. Crystal glasses sparkled and reflected the flames of the candles positioned in the centre of the table.

"This is a bit special," said Wayne, looking about admiringly.

"This is a special day," Grace answered, "The renovations are complete now."

Wayne sat at the table smelling fresh, his damp hair falling around his ears, his faded blue jeans rolled up and his feet bare. "No shoes or socks in the car," he said.

"I don't mind," Grace answered, hoping like mad that he would have nothing on at all by the end of the night.

Grace had cooked spaghetti marinara served with a green salad and a bottle of Pinot Gris. They sat and talked for ages after they had finished eating, both aware of the huge sexual tension between them. Wayne knew that if he made the move Grace would respond to him. There was a battle going on in his mind and he was weakening with every minute that passed. He decided he should just get up and go now without any more messing about.

"Okay, it's time for me to go," he said getting to his feet.

Grace stood also and slowly moved towards him. "Do you really want to go?"

"No, but I must or I might do something I shouldn't."

"Please don't go Wayne, not yet anyway."

She put her arms around his waist and moved her slender body towards his. He could feel her soft breasts against his hard chest and felt his desire for her rise.

"Let's have just one night together as we won't be seeing each other after today. That is unless your plumbing fails," she giggled.

"My plumbing never fails," he laughed. And it certainly didn't that night.

Wayne did not stay all night but went home in the early hours of the morning. He was glad Kathy was not in their bed because he was feeling really guilty.

He slept a few hours then got up to go to work without seeing Kathy. He had Grace on his mind all day and she was obviously thinking of him because she rang him around five to invite him over for a drink.

"I know I shouldn't see you again but I want to. Give me some time to think about this and I will ring you in a few days," he said.

Four days later he rang Grace and four weeks later he moved in with her.

Grace was the opposite of Kathy. Her dark hair, olive complexion and huge brown eyes fascinated Wayne and added to that she was almost as tall as him, slender and beautiful. She was a partner in a city law firm and was both articulate and smart. Grace had studied at university after leaving school and had worked hard, saving her money and working towards being independent. She owned the house Wayne was helping her to renovate and she loved making the house and garden her own.

"I'm putting my own stamp on it," she had told Wayne when he had questioned some of her unusual decisions. Wayne couldn't believe a woman like Grace could be interested in him but she was. Grace had fallen for Wayne the first time she laid eyes on him and as she got to know him and realised that he was kind and funny and clever, she knew he was the man she had been waiting for.

Confiding in one of her girlfriends she said. "When Wayne looked into my eyes the first time I felt something move inside me—I think it must have been my uterus contracting," she giggled.

Her friend gave her a quizzical look.

"Well it was in that area of my body, what else could it have been?"

"Wow," said her friend. "I have never had that happen to me."

"Every time I think about him I get a rush of desire. I think I will go mad if I don't have him."

"Boy, you have got it bad," said her friend.

"Yes, I have," she said thinking of Wayne again and feeling a rush of longing for him again.

Wayne avoided mentioning Kathy and his children and Grace didn't ask. She knew it was wrong, she knew she would hate it if someone did the same to her, but she couldn't help it, she loved him with an overwhelming desire that was driving her whole body and mind. It had changed her behaviour; she couldn't eat and she had lost weight. He was on her mind all the time. The way she felt about

Wayne was sometimes described in romantic novels and until now she had always thought it was an exaggeration.

Wayne still cared about Kathy but the Kathy he had known had disappeared into her ballooning body. She was more like a friend or a sister but she was certainly not his lover any more. He knew he would miss the children but they hardly ever saw him now anyway so they probably wouldn't notice a big difference. When he told Kathy he was leaving her she cried and begged him not to abandon her. She said she couldn't live without him and although he was sorry and sad, he left her anyway.

Wayne and Grace were very happy together and after being together for a year Grace became pregnant. When Kathy was told she was devastated because in her mind she had always thought Wayne would come back to her if or when she managed to lose weight or if he got tired of Grace.

Wayne sold their house and bought a smaller house for Kathy in Greenmount. He paid for everything except their weekly food, her mobile phone and petrol. He picked up the children every second Saturday morning and returned them to Kathy on Sunday afternoon. The twins seemed fine but Tommy never looked well and Grace urged Wayne to take him to see a paediatrician. Wayne didn't agree because Tommy always looked the same to him, and let it go.

When Tommy was rushed to hospital on three occasions with a severe asthma attack, Wayne raced in to see him. He questioned the staff about the Ventolin not being very effective because it always had been in the past, but he never imagined that Kathy would have withheld the Ventolin in order to see him. Tommy was given a referral to the asthma clinic within the hospital but Kathy did not follow through because she knew it was a waste of time. She racked her brains for ways to get Wayne's attention next and one day she knew what she had to do, and she went to the chemist to buy a few things.

6

Tommy

Flashing lights lit up the usually dark driveway. Quickly the paramedics entered the house to assess the patient and were kind and thorough, asking lots of questions as they took in the sad sight. A little three-year-old boy semi-conscious, pale, with slightly cyanosed lips and finger tips, no previous history of seizures, had been found by his mother lying in his cot having a seizure.

They applied an oxygen mask which improved his colour but he was very limp and not very responsive. He did not have a temperature so it did not seem like a febrile convulsion; his lungs were fine but his pulse was thready, so they put in an intravenous line to administer fluids and if necessary Valium if he began fitting again, and prepared to transport him to hospital.

Kathy was about to close the door behind her when one of the twins, who had been woken, came out to see what all the noise was about.

"Do you have other children in the house, Kathy?" asked the paramedic.

"Yes, two seven-year-olds."

"We can't leave them here alone."

"No — I wasn't thinking straight."

"Do you have anyone who can stay with the children, a neighbour perhaps?"

"No."

"Well I am sorry but we will have to take Tommy without you."

"No, please don't do that." Kathy did not want Tommy to go without her, and then she remembered Felicity Sharpe. She rang Felicity but her phone was turned off so she looked at the other phone numbers that she had scribbled down and remembered that Mandy had said she would be happy to babysit for her.

Mandy arrived ten minutes later and after the ambulance had departed she tucked the two confused little girls back into bed and sat in their room until they were fast asleep. Mandy found a blanket and lay on the couch watching television until she fell asleep.

In the morning Mandy was woken by Ruth and Amy who were already dressed in their school uniforms.

"You are both such good girls to get up and get ready for school on your own," said Mandy.

"We always get ourselves up and ready for school," said Amy.

"Well that's very grown up of you. What would you like for breakfast?"

"We've already had some bread and jam," said Ruth.

"You really are full of surprises," said Mandy. "You run and clean your teeth and I will make your lunches. What do you like in your sandwiches?"

"We only have jam or Vegemite," said Amy.

While the girls were in the bathroom cleaning their teeth, Mandy looked in the pantry and found tea, coffee, bread, jam and Vegemite. In the fridge there was milk, margarine and ice-cream. Mandy decided to go home and make a good lunch for the girls then take it to them at school before lunch time.

She took the girls to school and told them that she would bring their lunches to their classroom and also pick them up after school. The little girls seemed pleased and asked when their mother would be home again.

"I'm not sure, I'll ring her and when I pick you up I will be able to tell you. Have a nice day at school," said Mandy as she stood at the school gate watching the two little girls walk to their classroom with their big backpacks dwarfing their tiny frames.

Mandy rang Kathy's mobile several times and eventually got a reply. Kathy said she was not sure when they would be home as there were more tests to be done today and tomorrow.

"Well," said Mandy, "I am quite happy to look after your girls for a few days but I would prefer to have them at my place, is that okay with you?"

"Yes that's fine and thank you very much. I have to go now because my husband is here and the doctor is coming to talk to us." Kathy terminated the call without even saying goodbye and had not asked about the twins.

Mandy received a phone call about an hour later from the children's father, Wayne. He asked after Amy and Ruth and said he wanted to come and see the girls, and that he would pick them up from school that afternoon and bring them to Mandy. She gave him her address and he was there with the girls just after three-thirty. Wayne was the archetypal tall, dark and handsome tradie. His dark, wavy hair fell below his ears and he always had a smile on his face. He looked fit and in good shape and his lean, tanned body indicated a healthy lifestyle.

The two little girls were thrilled to be with their daddy and he sat down with one on each knee and kissed them in turn. "How are my little princesses?" he asked.

They both said they were fine and happy but would like Mummy to come home.

"She will be home on the weekend I think," he told them.

"How many days is that?" Amy asked.

"Only two more, but I will come and get you and take you with me for the whole weekend, then you can go back to Mummy on Sunday night like you usually do."

Wayne spoke to Mandy out of earshot of the girls. He told her this was the fourth time he had been called to the hospital because of Tommy but this time it was for a different reason. It was not his asthma but a seizure of some sort and it was being investigated by a neurologist.

"I'm worried about him but now that he is in hospital I'm sure it will all be sorted out by the medical staff."

Mandy looked at Wayne and noticed how worried he seemed. He had dark rings under his eyes and she suspected he had not been sleeping well.

"Try not to worry too much, I doubt that he will be discharged until the cause of the seizure has been investigated and diagnosed properly," she said. She thought of some of the dreadful things that could cause a seizure in a child and hoped like hell it was none of them.

Wayne stayed and had dinner with his girls then as he left he thanked Mandy and offered her money to cover the cost of the children's stay. Mandy refused, saying she was only too pleased that she could help care for the girls. Wayne organised to pick up his daughters on Friday after work and thanked her again.

Mandy closed the door after Wayne and said to herself, 'This is so sad; I am a stranger to these little girls and yet both their parents are quite happy to leave them with me, they don't know anything about me but two of their most precious little ones are in my care, poor little darlings. I think I had better get in touch with Felicity Sharpe tomorrow.'

7

Felicity

Following Mandy's phone call, Felicity went to Kathy's home on Monday morning and found no one at home. She was just about to leave when Kathy's car pulled into the driveway.

"Hello Kathy, I heard your little Tommy has been in hospital again. I am here to offer a helping hand if you need it," she said in a friendly tone.

"I think I'm okay," said Kathy, pulling shopping bags out of the car boot.

Felicity noticed that Tommy was not with her and asked, "Is Tommy still in hospital?"

"No, he was discharged yesterday."

"Oh good! Where is he, Kathy?"

"Inside."

"Did you leave him on his own?" she asked, concerned now.

"Yes, but he is asleep and I have only been out for five minutes."

'Yeah, five minutes my foot,' muttered Felicity under her breath as she viewed the bags from a supermarket which was at least a ten-minute drive from Kathy's home.

They were standing at the front door and Kathy seemed reluctant to open the door. Felicity was worried about Tommy so she stood her ground, making it very obvious that she wanted to go inside. Eventually Kathy opened the door and Felicity followed her in. The house was quiet and dark, the blinds were closed, otherwise everything looked okay.

"Would you like me to open the blinds while you go and check on Tommy?" asked Felicity.

As Kathy went to the bedroom Felicity opened the blinds very quickly then hurried after Kathy into Tommy's room, where he was asleep in his cot. The room was dark and cool but Tommy was covered up and did not stir. They left the sleeping little boy who was quietly snoring and went to the kitchen.

"Did you find out what caused the seizure?" asked Felicity.

"No, the doctors were baffled and just told me to bring him back if it happens again."

"Well let's hope it doesn't happen again. You must be relieved to be home."

"Yes," said Kathy cutting short any further conversation. She just wanted Felicity out of her home.

Felicity left the house. She was not very happy about what she had seen but was not sure exactly why. It was not only that Tommy had been left in the house alone or Kathy's apparent lack of concern and casual manner, it was something else she just felt was not quite right.

"Just ring me if you need me," Felicity said to Kathy as she climbed into her car. The vision of Tommy deeply asleep in that dark room was imprinted on her mind. She made a quick phone call to Mandy telling her what she had discovered when she'd gone to Kathy's house. Mandy agreed that the situation was worrying and said she would continue to help in any way she could.

"I am going to consult one of my colleagues at the Medical Centre about this," Felicity said to Mandy.

8

Café

The following week the women met for coffee and a chat at the usual time. Mandy said she had sent Kathy a message telling her they were meeting today but was not expecting her to come because of Tommy's trip to hospital.

Jane was a bit more relaxed and talkative than usual and gave the impression that she wanted to be more involved with the other two. She told them that before moving to Greenmount she had lived by the sea and when asked where exactly, both the women were surprised to hear that it was the wealthy seaside suburb of Brighton.

"It must have been difficult to leave the beach, and Brighton is such a nice suburb," said Astrid.

"Yes it was very difficult to move because I had lived in the area all my life and I really miss the beach. I could watch the sunset over the bay from my living room windows and I certainly miss that. Plus I left behind a large group of friends, some I had known since childhood."

Jane thought of the wide expanse of glass in her Brighton living room which had been a source of pleasure every afternoon as the sun went down over Port Phillip Bay. She had never tired of the view and it was one of the things she missed most about her previous life. That and her frequent walks along the foreshore or out to the end of the pier whatever the weather.

"Your friends can be here for a visit in just over an hour," Astrid said.

"Yes," sighed Jane, "That's if they bother to make the effort."

The thread of conversation came to a halt as the door of the café opened and Kathy walked in.

"Hello Kathy, we didn't expect to see you. How is Tommy?" asked Mandy.

"He's good," she replied.

"Come and sit down, we have just ordered coffee. What would you like?"

"I'll get it," she said and walked to the counter.

"Oh dear, I hope she hasn't left Tommy at home alone again," whispered Mandy to the others. "Should I say something to her about it?"

"Let's give her a moment; she probably has someone babysitting," Astrid answered.

When Kathy returned to the table the small talk resumed and eventually got around to Tommy.

"Is Tommy okay now?" asked Jane.

"Yes, much better," Kathy answered.

"Who is looking after him at the moment?" Astrid asked kindly.

"He's alright, he's asleep."

"Kathy, he's not alone again is he?" asked Mandy.

"Yes but he's okay."

"What if he wakes and you're not there, or if he is sick again, or if the house burns down or anything?" said Mandy.

"I don't see what is wrong with leaving him asleep in his cot. My mother always left me alone when I was little. I know he won't wake up."

"How do you know that he won't wake up?"

"I just do, I know my son."

Mandy took a deep breath and straightened her shoulders.

"Look Kathy, you can say it's none of my business but I am worried about Tommy. He's recently been in hospital, he's a little boy and little children really should never be left alone under any circumstances."

"Well, I've only been away for ten minutes and I'm going home now." She stood up to leave, her face flushed and she was obviously flustered. "Bye," she said and quickly left. Her coffee was untouched.

"Oh my god," said Mandy, "I'm really worried about those children and Kathy, she obviously has some big problems. I wish I had her ex-husband's phone number but it never occurred to me that I would need to speak to him again."

"We should pass this on to Felicity," said Jane.

"I have already spoken to her about Kathy and I know she paid her a visit," said Mandy. She took out her phone. "I'll leave her a message now to get in touch with me."

"Felicity definitely needs an update on Kathy," said Jane.

Astrid nodded in agreement.

9

Seizure

Exactly two weeks after the first seizure, Tommy had another one. Mandy had just sat down to watch a movie with her husband John when the phone rang.

"Damn, I don't feel like talking to anyone tonight, can you answer it John and if it's for me say I am in bed asleep."

"I'll answer it but you know I am no good at telling lies."

John answered the phone and handed it to Mandy. "The twins need you again," he said.

"Hello," said Mandy.

"Hi Mandy, this is Jan Short the paramedic you met at Kathy's place a fortnight ago. Tommy needs to go to hospital again and I am hoping you can come here to take care of the twins. Kathy is reluctant to ring you, that's why I'm asking."

"I'm on my way." She grabbed her car keys and walked quickly to the front door. "Sorry John, but I have to go. I'll ring you when I can."

"Why don't you bring them here tonight, then at least you can sleep in your own bed instead of her couch?"

"Okay, good idea, I will," she replied.

The lights on the ambulance were flashing when Mandy arrived.

Kathy, who was sitting in the front with the driver, barely glanced at Mandy, keeping her eyes looking down at her lap.

"I'll take the girls to my place," Mandy called through the partly opened window. Kathy nodded, keeping her eyes averted.

Mandy entered the house half expecting the two little girls to greet her but they were in bed asleep. There was a night light on the chest of drawers in their bedroom enabling her to see the children. She spoke to them and said she was there to take them to her place but they did not stir. Mandy gave each of them a gentle push hoping to wake them but still they remained asleep. She spoke loudly and moved them more vigorously, expecting to rouse them, but still there was not much response. She put on the light and made further attempts to wake them but quickly realised they were deeply asleep and could have been sedated. Mandy turned the girls on to their sides and checked their breathing and pulses, which in both children were normal.

She went to the kitchen and searched in the cupboards until she found what she was looking for. There were three bottles, one unopened, another half full, and in the rubbish bin there was an empty bottle. The three bottles were labelled Phenergan. In the kitchen sink were teaspoons and several small medicine cups.

What on earth is Kathy doing? What can she be thinking, Mandy thought to herself. This must be how she knows Tommy will not wake when she leaves him at home asleep. She said she knew her son but what she should have said is that he wouldn't wake up for a few hours because he couldn't.

Mandy rang John to tell him she would have to stay at the house with Ruth and Amy because they had been sedated, and he suggested she ring Felicity. Once again, just like the last time she had tried to call Felicity at night, she did not answer her phone, so Mandy left a message.

Mandy continued to keep an eye on the girls knowing they would eventually be rousable. She checked their breathing and heart rate as well as their colour every half hour and did not try to sleep because she was worried and extremely angry. Sometime after midnight Ruth woke up and began crying for her mother. Mandy went in to comfort her and the crying woke Amy. She took them both to the toilet and gave them a drink of water then settled them in bed and back to sleep.

In the morning Mandy asked the girls if they had been given any medicine last night.

"Yes we had Tommy's pink magic-dream medicine. Mummy mixes it with ice-cream."

"Does Mummy give it to you very often?"

"No, only sometimes."

"Does she give it to Tommy very often?"

"Yes, all the time, Mummy says he needs it."

"Okay, let's get you two dressed and we will go to my house. You needn't go to school today, we will do something nice at my place. How about some cooking together instead, would you like that?"

Both the girls were pleased at the thought of being with Mandy.

"Mummy won't let us cook," said Amy.

Halfway through the morning Mandy received a call from Felicity. "Sorry I wasn't awake last night when you rang, how can I help you?"

"Felicity, I am extremely worried about Kathy and all three children now. Tommy is in hospital again and I have the girls with me once more. When I went there last night they were sedated and they tell me their mother sedates Tommy often."

"Oh my goodness, that's terrible" responded Felicity. I'll get in touch with the hospital. Thank you Mandy, leave it with me."

As Mandy put the phone down she said to herself, "that's what you said last time, Felicity." She found it hard to accept waiting for someone to intervene; she worried that something awful could happen, but at the same time she knew one had to be careful when dealing with parents and their children.

10

Amy and Ruth

Amy and Ruth were identical twins, pretty little girls with their mother's blonde hair and their father's brown eyes. They were thin and pale-skinned with a smattering of freckles across their slightly upturned noses. Thank goodness they had each other because what they had to endure would have been impossible to cope with alone. They clung to each other emotionally and frequently they could be seen huddled together, arms around the other's shoulders. At school they were always together, playing alongside other children but never separating from each other. They could both read well and their understanding of numbers and ability to spell was average, so apart from the jam sandwiches their teacher was not concerned about them. The teacher had plenty of noisy students taking up her time and attention. She knew the twins were quiet but as they were always well behaved they did not get any special consideration. If one of them was upset the other took on the mothering role and comforted her sister, making an effort to remain dry-eyed even though often the bottom lip would quiver.

They often slept in the same bed, keeping each other warm and freeing the other bed for their mother to sleep in. Their doll's house was their escape as it provided a safe, secure, pretend home where there was always a mummy and a daddy dancing attention on the two little twin dolls who lived there. Their storyline would always be the same: mummy and daddy both at home, sitting on the couch together, having dinner together or playing a game with the two of them. Just normal things which they craved.

11

Eva and Martha

Eva was expecting her mother to arrive home in an ambulance about 10am. Everything was prepared for her homecoming. Two weeks ago, Eva had endured a grilling from the staff at the rehab hospital who seemed to think she would be unable to care for her mother. Eva did not want to make a fuss or tell them that she had trained as a nurse and knew a great deal about basic nursing so she just answered their questions and asked the questions she needed answered. There were a few things she had to get before her mother could come home and several things to organise. She purchased a ripple mattress, had safety rails installed in the bathroom, bought a wheelchair and made sure the local doctor would be willing to visit her mother at home and, with Felicity's assistance, organised someone to shower her mother several days a week to give her a bit of a break.

Eva's mother Martha arrived with a smile on her face after giggling at the two ambulance men who carried her up the stairs. They settled her into the new wheelchair waiting for her in the living room. She had a beautiful view of the nearby mountains and commented that it was an improvement on the view of a brick wall she had been looking at for the past few months. Eva, wanting to please her mother, had placed a vase of flowers, a glass of water, a few magazines and her mother's bible on the table within reach. Martha looked at the contents of the table and said, "You do know me very well Eva, and I am so glad to be out of that place and with you. I know you will look after me, I hope I won't be too much of a nuisance though."

"You are not a nuisance. Let's have a cup of coffee, I know you would love a cup now, wouldn't you. And I have made some biscuits," she added.

"Yes please, and without sugar; they kept giving me sugar in my tea and coffee no matter how many times I said no sugar."

Martha was well and truly settled in by the end of the week and asked when her two sons were coming to see her.

"I don't know but I will give them a ring tonight and see what they say," Eva replied. "As far as I am concerned they are welcome at any time."

Eva's brothers were both married to women who Eva didn't get on with, particularly Jacky, who had booked Martha into the nursing home. She didn't see them often because it had caused an argument but she expected her brothers would visit their mother in spite of that.

No one was living at Martha's house and Eva went every week to check on it and collect her mother's mail. When entering the house Eva saw at once that certain pieces of Martha's antique furniture had been removed from the bedroom and living room. It did not look as though there had been a break-in, more like someone had let themselves in with a key. Eva knew at once that it would have been one of her brothers. When she went home and told her mother, Martha was extremely annoyed.

"Well if they can move my dressing table I might as well have it here, don't you think?" she said crossly. It had sentimental value to Martha as it had belonged to her mother, to whom Martha had been extremely close. That dressing table had sat in the same place in the house for years and years. Martha's parents had left the house to Martha and she had left all the beautiful old pieces of furniture in exactly the same places her parents had kept them. The dressing table had a large mirror encased in an elaborately carved wooden frame above a wide, marble-topped table. There were four heavy drawers where her mother kept her bed linen and towels. In the top drawer she stored her handkerchiefs, gloves and perfume. As a little girl Eva had been lifted up to sit on the cold marble to watch her mother in front of the mirror powdering her nose and putting her hair up and then in turn to have her own hair brushed and braided.

With these memories on her mind Eva said, "Yes that's true. I'll ring to see which one of them has it and get him to bring it here."

"And you can tell him that I am not dead yet and I did not give him permission to take anything from my house," Martha snapped.

It was not easy to get the dressing table moved to Eva's house—in fact it took three months and more than a dozen phone calls before Eva's brother begrudgingly delivered the treasured piece of furniture to his mother. As he was leaving he said to Eva, "I'll have it back when she has finished with it."

Eva told her mother what her brother had said and asked, "What do you want me to do with it later?"

"Keep it and do what you want with it."

Eva knew at once that she would eventually give it to one of her children.

Life rolled along day by day, week by week, until one day Eva's husband Martin came home to find Allen and Jacky's daughters sitting in the kitchen talking to Martha. One of the girls kept saying over and over, "but Nana why won't you sell your house?"

Martha, who was holding a letter in her hand, answered with determination, "It's all I have and when I die it can be sold and then your parents will get their share, not before."

"But why Nana, why won't you sell it now? Mum and Dad need the money now, you've read the letter?" continued the nagging grandchild.

When Martin overheard the conversation and the girl repeating "why Nana, why?" he stepped in and said, "She said no and that's all there is to it."

The two girls got up and left in a huff, leaving behind the incriminating letter their mother had written begging Martha to sell her house to get them out of a financial hole. It was the last straw. They had done silly things before but this was really nasty and it caused an even bigger rift in the family. Poor Martha, she had endured so much in her long life and all she wanted now was to live out her remaining years in peace and quiet.

All Martha's life she had read her bible before going to sleep. It was something passed down from her parents but her daughter Eva had not taken up the habit.

"Gee Mum, you must have read that from cover to cover a dozen times or more by now, don't you get sick of it?" Eva asked.

"No I don't and I wish you would do a bit more bible reading. It helps to settle the mind and gives some clarity to life," Martha replied.

Eva had some smart answers on the tip of her tongue but decided to let it go. Instead she said, "When I was a little girl and still brainwashed I was religious, if you remember."

"Yes I remember, but that was not being brainwashed. I would listen to you saying your prayers before going to sleep, do you remember? Gentle Jesus, meek and mild, look upon a little child," Martha recited.

"Yes, I remember, but I found a lot of that religious stuff a bit scary at times, all that 'be good or else you won't go to heaven' business was terrifying, particularly because you were always telling me that I was naughty."

"What do you mean?"

Eva sat down next to her mother and began to tell her about a very vivid memory she had of a day in the garden. Eva had been about nine years old and she and her young brother were helping Martha rake leaves and pull up weeds to take around to the back yard to burn off in the incinerator. Everyone used to burn off garden rubbish in those days and autumn afternoons were often full of the smell of burning leaves and smoke hanging in the air. It was late on one of those autumn afternoons the sun was halfway down the sky and the air was filled with smoke haze. Eva had stopped raking or weeding some time ago as she had collected a handful of large wriggling worms which she now kindly put back into a hole she had dug in the garden. She was imagining how happy the worms would be back in their earthly homes. She was pleased with herself for not harming them, knowing that her brother would have happily chopped them into little pieces. A blackbird which had been scratching in the garden nearby suddenly chirped loudly as the family cat appeared from around the side of the house. Eva was roused from her daydream and stood up abruptly, turning around to see the sun which, because of the smoke and the movement of the autumn clouds, looked strange and eerie. It seemed to be whirling fast and the colour was different. It was quiet and she was alone and she was scared. She looked for her mother and brother for reassurance but they were not there, they had disappeared.

Oh no, it's happened, the second coming: Jesus has come back to earth and all the good people have gone with him and the bad ones have been left behind, she panicked. Eva screamed and ran as fast as she could around the side of the house towards the back door so that she could get inside away from the bad things that she imagined would be trying to get her, and there she saw her mother in the back yard calmly feeding the incinerator with weeds and cuttings from the garden. Her young brother was pretending to be an American Indian, dancing around the incinerator making hooting and hollering noises.

Martha stared at her now adult daughter and said, "I don't remember that."

"Mum, I thought Jesus had come, I thought I had been left behind with all the sinners; it was awful. Are you sure you can't remember that?" said Eva to her mother.

"No not really—what did I do?" asked Martha.

"You laughed at me and told me not to be silly and not to take it so literally or something similar."

"Did I give you a hug?"

"No." Under her breath she said to herself 'you rarely hugged me.'

"Come here and I will hug you now," she said. "I know I was not always the best mother to you, those years after your father died were very difficult."

Eva hugged her mother and silently agreed it had been extremely difficult and it had affected all of them in various ways. Martha had not been the best mother because she had been chronically depressed and just managed to cope, sometimes not coping but pushing herself to the limit. She tried not to show her feelings to her children thinking that was best, but it only taught them that their feelings were not important, and so they learnt not to express their feelings, and a hug was very unusual.

On the day that Eva's father had died the children were taken by kind neighbours and cared for until after the funeral. Eva was only away for about three days but it felt like three weeks to her. She was not sent to school and had none of her own toys or books so she spent the days walking aimlessly around the house and garden trying to understand why she was there and not at home. After dinner the pious Catholic family knelt in front of their shabby chairs and said Hail Marys with rosary beads, something Eva had found profoundly strange. They did, however, include Eva and her family in their prayers. The day after the funeral—which Eva had not attended—she was finally allowed back to her own home. She still had not been told what had happened to her father or why she had to stay away from her own home.

Home at last, Eva stood in her own bedroom listening to the birds singing their end of day chorus in the large palm trees next door. It was as regular as the sun coming up and going down each day; hundreds of common sparrows and starlings sang their morning or evening songs, a sound which was as normal to Eva as her own heartbeat.

Her mother Martha came in to the room and, lacking any preamble, said, "Your father has gone to be with his mother." Then without even touching Eva she turned and left the room. Eva stared at a keyhole on the chest of drawers; a strange awareness of something she had been trying to keep at bay was creeping into mind. She thought to herself. 'Daddy's mother is dead, Daddy must be dead.' Next door the choir of hundreds of birds continued. Tears stung Eva's eyes as she tried very hard to be like her mother and not cry. She stayed in her room until she had her emotions under control as she had been taught, then emerged to find her brother.

All in all Eva had not had a happy childhood and she wished she could have had a closer relationship with her mother. Now as an adult she understood that her mother had been doing what she had thought best and had definitely been struggling to care for her children on her own and stay sane at the same time.

12

Jane

Jane began to enjoy the company of Mandy and Astrid who were both very different to the friends she had left behind. She could not remember ever hearing her friend Pixie saying anything sympathetic or complimentary about anyone: rather she mostly talked about herself and loved to gossip about everyone. Jane's new friends seemed grounded and unpretentious and always found something interesting and informative to talk about and seemed to care about each other's wellbeing. Except for Astrid, Mandy, Felicity and Kathy, she didn't really know anyone else in Greenmount yet and was limited in where she could go and what she could do because she and her husband had only one car between them—her car, which he drove to work. It didn't worry her too much because she knew walking was good exercise and she couldn't afford gym fees at the moment. Walking to the school and the shops was enjoyable and the café where they met not far from the school was in the local shopping strip.

Jane hoped to find a part-time job and had been checking the local paper weekly and looking out for signs in the shop windows. She was really looking for a position in a boutique or something of that sort. When nothing in the small shops came up she decided it would have to be the local supermarket because she really needed to earn some money. On this particular day before meeting Mandy and Astrid, she had left her CV with the manager at the supermarket and walked to the café. She had hoped for an interview at the supermarket and was more dressed up than usual, looking very elegant in a dusky pink cashmere tunic, slimline black pants, black high-heeled boots and wearing a string of sleek black pearls and ear rings to match. She knew how to take full advantage of her expensive leftover wardrobe and being slim and reasonably tall, everything looked good on her.

The other two arrived and they sat and talked for an hour, drinking their coffee and sharing one cake between the three of them. Mandy filled them in on the Kathy drama and once again they all expressed that they were worried about Kathy and her children.

"Jane, you look lovely today," commented Astrid. "Have you been out or are you going somewhere?"

Jane explained that she wanted a part-time job and had dressed up hoping for an interview. "I won't hold my breath though, I didn't even get to see the manager. A woman at the office took my CV and said that they had quite a number of people ahead of me on their books looking for work already."

Astrid gazed at Jane's throat. "Those pearls you are wearing are stunning," she said. "Are they real?"

"Yes they are, they are from Broome in Western Australia. My husband had some business over there and brought pearls back for me each time he went."

"Next time he goes can I put in an order?" joked Astrid.

"That won't be happening anytime soon," Jane replied with a sigh.

"What work does he do here?" asked Mandy.

"Well, I would rather not say. I don't want to be impolite, I just find it difficult to talk about it." Jane really did not want to appear rude; she wasn't proud of her husband or where he was working and she decided to keep it to herself for now. She had almost blurted out her reason for moving away from Brighton a few times but managed to keep it to herself.

"I will probably tell you all about it one day when we are talking openly, I just need time. I enjoy talking to you all and find these meetings we have together are like group therapy, don't you think?"

"Yes it's wonderful to have other women to meet with and let off some steam," said Astrid. "We are here for you whenever you need to talk."

To move the conversation along she said. "Are you walking to the school after we leave here?"

"Yes, I'll walk with you," Jane replied.

Jane was doing her best to adjust to her new life. Although the children were happy and her health was good, her world as she had known it had crashed and hit rock bottom, the life of privilege and wealth had gone and she knew she would never get it back. She knew she would manage but she needed time to get used to everything.

Jane had lived with her husband and two children in a huge house within walking distance of the bay. They had their own swimming pool, tennis court, gardener and twice-weekly cleaner. She and her husband, Rick, drove expensive European cars, the children went to the best private school in the area and their holidays were either in the snow fields or overseas. Before the children were born, Jane had worked as personal assistant to Rick, who was an accountant. Rick's company merged with another group so he had three partners and a larger staff. There was always plenty of money and Jane bought anything and everything she wanted for herself and her family.

For almost ten years everything appeared to be wonderful. Jane went to the gym every second day and ran along the foreshore the other days. She met up with friends for lunch several times a week, joined a book club, entertained at home at least once a month, subscribed to the

Australian Ballet and Melbourne Theatre Company and volunteered in an organisation which assisted underprivileged women to dress and apply for work. She was busy and she was very happy.

The first sign that something was wrong was when Rick began to have trouble sleeping more than three hours a night. He also began drinking a lot more than usual and his face began to show obvious signs of stress. Jane asked him what was worrying him but he would not tell her and if she persisted, he lost his temper and swore at her and slammed doors. She tried to get him to see their doctor but that also made him angry, so she was at a loss. When the cause of his despair was revealed it was the last thing she suspected.

It was a warm summer evening; the day had been scorching hot but a cool change had blown in from the south. Jane had promised to take the children to buy an ice-cream and eat it walking along the sea shore where they could jump in the water, pick up shells or just run around in circles if they wanted to. They loved the beach. There was a knock at the front door just as they just finished dinner. Jane opened the door and was greeted by two plainclothes detectives who asked to come in to see Rick. They went into Rick's study and after a short time emerged with Rick, telling her he was under arrest for embezzlement from the company he co-owned. He was taken into custody and remained there until his lawyer could have him bailed.

Rick spent two years in jail, the house and cars were sold to pay debts and help reimburse the company, and Jane and the children moved out of the area so they would not have to see anyone they knew. Jane's parents urged her to divorce Rick but she still loved him in spite of what he had done and decided to stick by him and wait for him. In an effort to get right away from Brighton she moved into a two-bedroom flat in a suburb on the other side of Melbourne, enrolled the children in the local state primary school and found a job in a large department store in the city. Eventually Rick's parents and her parents gave Jane enough money to put a deposit on an inexpensive house in Greenmount so when Rick came out of jail they all moved there.

With assistance, Rick was able to get a job at the abattoir, which he hated, but it was better than being in jail. He knew he was lucky to have Jane by his side but he had a lot of trouble adjusting to their different lifestyle. He was angry with himself for what he had done and angrier that he had been caught. He was an arrogant man who really considered himself better than everyone else and did not get on with the men he worked with now because he considered them his inferiors. All day he dreamt up ways of getting back to his old life but the things he needed were money and contacts. No one would lend him money and his old contacts did not want to know him now. There was just one way he might be able to escape his hellish existence and he decided to give it a try.

13

Astrid

For the first time in a long while Astrid was feeling unencumbered and settled. By moving to Greemount she had been able to escape from an extremely painful part of her old life. Besides her ex-husband, the main thing she had wanted to escape from was her parents and now that she had been able to put more distance between them, she felt relieved.

When she was a child her family had appeared to be the epitome of perfection to the outside world but it was all a lie. Her father, Gus, ruled the family with threats, violence and abuse. Her mother, Pam, was weak and went along with everything he did just to keep the peace. His abuse was physical, emotional and sexual.

Astrid escaped from home as soon as she finished school and began a nursing degree. She had a job working in a bar at nights and the weekends and shared accommodation with other students. After graduation she married a young man called Norman who was a carpenter. They bought a little house in Footscray and began to renovate it. Several years into the marriage they had a daughter they named Julie. Following Julie's birth Astrid suffered from post-natal depression and severe anxiety. On the advice of her doctor she began seeing a psychologist on a weekly basis. It was during these sessions that Astrid uncovered her fear that she could not protect her daughter from her husband, father, grandfather or, for that matter, any other man. When prompted by the psychologist she began to reveal memories that she had suppressed and tried to keep hidden for years. Her father had sexually abused her from a very young age and her mother had seemed oblivious to his treatment of her. He had told Astrid it was his duty as her father to teach her these special things. The innocent child had no choice but to accept her father's disgusting behaviour.

Astrid learnt to go to a special place in the jungle on her bedroom curtains. The flowering trees were lush and green with happy monkeys and coloured birds sitting in the branches smiling at her, encouraging her to stay with them in the safety of the verdant foliage. After each ordeal was over she would go outside and climb into her tree house which was high up in a big pine tree in the back garden. Her mother would come home from church and call for Astrid to come and help set the table for lunch. She always tried to hide up in the tree but her mother knew she was there and would climb up to growl at her and demand that she help with lunch. When the family sat down to eat their Sunday roast her father would tell them to hold hands around the table as he thanked the lord for the food on the table and the wonderful life they enjoyed. Astrid always tried to sit between her brother and her mother so she did not have to touch her father or he touch her again. She hated Sundays.

Sometimes the family went to stay with Gus's parents on the Mornington Peninsula and because it was so far away they usually stayed for the whole weekend. During these visits Astrid was abused by her grandfather. Her grandfather was a big tall man who was adored by his wife and three sons. He was a well-known businessman who was liked and respected in the local area.

As a little girl Astrid had been taught to respect and obey adults and she therefore felt she had to do what he said. Anything she told her mother was ignored as exaggeration or telling lies.

Astrid's brother Robert was also subjected to cruel and violent treatment from their father. He criticised and belittled the boy constantly and beat him for the slightest thing. Their mother rarely intervened because if she did, she was mistreated also. It was a quiet household because Pam and the children were scared to say anything for fear of upsetting Gus. The saying 'walking on egg shells' was the best way to describe their life at home.

When Astrid was fourteen she decided to put a lock on her bedroom door thinking this would keep her father out. When he discovered the lock he was furious and removed the whole door then beat Astrid. This was when she decided she would have to leave home as soon as she could and saw finishing school as the time of escape. That was still at least two years away though and she wondered many times if she could last that long.

The memories which were revealed when Astrid saw the psychologist were so painful and difficult to cope with that they caused a rift between Astrid and Norman, and their marriage did not survive. They were divorced before Julie started school.

A year ago, Astrid attended the funeral of an elderly aunt and reconnected with Marjorie, a cousin of her mother's whom she had not seen since she was a little girl. They got on very well together and began a friendship that both of them treasured. Cousin Marjorie lived in Greenmount and invited Astrid to visit her and stay for the weekend, which she did several times.

They talked endlessly and discovered that in spite of the age difference they had a lot in common. Both loved gardening and reading and both were artistic and loved the outdoors. On one such occasion Marjorie asked Astrid if she would like to come and live with her, saying that they could help each other out in many ways.

Marjorie had been a teacher and had two children who were both working overseas so she craved the company of family. The thought of Astrid and Julie living with her made her very happy. When they moved in everything fell into place. Astrid helped with the gardening and housework and Marjorie did the cooking and washing. When Astrid was working, Marjorie cared for Julie, taking her and picking her up from school. Marjorie began to teach Julie to cook and they often cooked the evening meal together.

For Astrid's birthday, Julie made a cake for her mother and iced it with Marjorie's help. After dinner, while they were enjoying the cake, Marjorie said, "Astrid there is a letter for you, it's from your mother. It's probably a birthday card."

Astrid paid little attention to the letter and only opened it because Julie wanted to see the card. It was a birthday card with a short note asking Astrid to pay them a visit because they had something very important to discuss with her.

"I am too busy to visit them at the moment, they will just have to wait."

The following week Astrid's mother rang and spoke to Marjorie. She explained that there was some money for Julie but they could only give it to Astrid after discussing something very important with her. She asked Marjorie to try to persuade Astrid to visit them, but she was not easily swayed and was still reluctant to go. Next time they were together without Julie, Marjorie said, "I know you are not very close to your parents but this could be to your financial advantage."

"You're right," replied Astrid. I am not close to them; I hate them and I don't want to see them."

"Hate them—that's a bit harsh, isn't it?"

"Well if you knew the truth you would not think it was harsh."

Marjorie did not know about Astrid's childhood and did not want to pry so she thought she should say no more.

A few weeks passed and Astrid's Uncle Joe rang and spoke severely to Astrid and somehow managed to persuade her to make time to visit her parents on the Mornington Peninsula, where they now lived in the house Gus had inherited from his parents.

14

Astrid's Parents

It took Astrid about two hours to reach her parents' home. It was an easy drive because the freeway took her most of the way. As she drove she listened to her favourite talkback radio presenter on the ABC which helped to distract her from thoughts of her parents and why she had given in and agreed to visit them. She calculated that she would have to leave there by 2pm to be home at four to take Julie for her piano lesson. Of course Marjorie would take Julie if she was late but her parents didn't know that and she was not going to tell them anything about her arrangements at home.

She had butterflies in her tummy and her mouth was dry as she arrived just after midday and sat down with her parents on an old wooden balcony overlooking the garden. The balcony was very high and gave them a wonderful view of the sea. It was supported by tall timber poles and beneath was an attractive native garden where honey eaters and spinebills were flitting from branch to branch dipping their long beaks into the colourful flowers. Astrid did not touch either of her parents and she kept her distance so they could not touch her. Gus was in a wheelchair because he had suffered a stroke the previous year and although he had recovered to some degree, he was still having trouble walking very far.

"We don't use the wheelchair all the time; in fact usually only when we go out but sometimes your father's bad leg plays up and it just seems safer to use the chair on those days," Pam told her.

Astrid did not reply because she didn't care that he was unable to walk properly, in fact she was glad to see him so sad and pathetic, looking old and stuck in a wheelchair. Serves him right, she thought to herself.

Pam had made a pot of tea and a plate of sandwiches which she placed on the table. "I'm not staying," she said. "I'm going out for an hour, your father has something to tell you so I'll leave you two alone to talk."

"I have to leave by two," said Astrid, horrified at the thought of being in the company of her father with no one to act as a buffer. "Do you have to go?"

"Yes. I have an appointment which I must attend but I will be back before then," said her mother.

Once again Astrid felt a moment of panic at the thought of being alone with her father but quickly realised she had nothing to fear from him now—in fact she had the upper hand. Despite that, her hand was unsteady as she poured the tea for herself and her father. She bit into one of the sandwiches while she waited for him to speak. When Gus eventually spoke his speech was slightly slurred but Astrid had no trouble understanding him.

"What I want to discuss with you is that your mother and I would like to have a relationship with our granddaughter Julie."

Putting the sandwich back onto her plate, Astrid said nothing.

"She is our granddaughter and we have a right to know her and I'm sure she would like to know us."

Astrid almost choked on the bread in her mouth as anger rose within.

"We have not seen her since she was born," he added.

Astrid swallowed the bread with difficulty, she was furious but still managed to remain silent.

"We have quite a bit of money to leave to you and your brother but we don't feel we should leave it to you if we can't see Julie."

Astrid could not control herself any longer. She got to her feet and stood over her father.

"You do not deserve to see my daughter and you never will," she raged at him.

Seemingly untouched by her outburst, Gus said, "We know that you are not well off and we could help you out by giving you the money."

"Do you think I will be bought with your filthy money after what you did to me?" Astrid yelled furiously at her father. "You don't deserve to have a granddaughter and I wouldn't trust you with her even if you were paralysed from the neck down. You disgust me and I can't even bear the thought of Julie being in the same room with you."

"Come on," he said, "what are you talking about?"

"You know very well what I'm talking about, you molested me."

"I don't know what you are talking about, that was nothing, you were just a child. You have to let that go, forget it, that was years ago. It was nothing."

"NOTHING? It was not nothing! You stole my innocence, my childhood. You made my life difficult and you spoiled any chance of a normal relationship with a man. You are the reason my marriage failed."

Astrid moved closer to her father. She was a tall woman and she towered over him. He looked up at her, squinting as the strong sun almost blinded him. Raising his hand to protect his eyes he said, "Don't be ridiculous," and made an awkward attempt to laugh at her.

Astrid was so angry she turned and kicked at the wheelchair but missed, her shoe connecting with the timber railing on the balcony causing it to splinter, and several pieces fell into the garden below.

"What are you doing, you fool," yelled her father, "you have broken it."

"I don't care," she yelled back at him.

As Astrid turned to go her father said, "Move me closer to the railing so I can pull it back into position."

She was tempted to walk off and leave him fuming but instead she turned and wheeled him towards the railing.

"Can you at least give what I said some thought, Astrid. It would mean a great deal to your mother as well as me."

"I'm going, and I'm not going to think about it at all and I don't want your fucking money ever," Astrid shouted at him as she descended the stairs and ran to her car.

The bastard, how could he ask such a thing, she thought. He had been a dreadful father and her mother a not much better parent. She hated them both and wished she had not gone to see them. She had known it was a mistake; she should have stuck to her guns no matter what her uncle had said to her. She thought of herself and her brother as little children and began to cry. She could see the two of them hiding in their tree-house, huddled together sobbing and scared, hoping their parents wouldn't look for them up there. They had been powerless and abused by the two people who should have loved and protected them. She really did hate them so much.

Driving back to Greenmount she put on a Pink Floyd CD so loud she couldn't even hear herself think.

15

Mandy

Mandy had retired from nursing several years ago following a nasty incident that occurred at the hospital where she had worked for thirty years. A burned child had died on the night shift after Mandy had cared for her on the previous afternoon shift. Mandy had loved her job and took it very seriously. She cared very much about what she did and tried to always do the best for her patients. Her colleagues blamed her for the death and she was treated very badly. She was denied counselling initially, ignored and given very bad advice in the following days because no one seemed to care. She felt no one was worried about the child's death except the girl's parents and herself. The junior medical staff remained silent and the senior doctors could not agree on why the child had died. Mandy suffered post-traumatic stress disorder and found daily life difficult. She lost weight, couldn't sleep and was constantly bursting into tears, the slightest upset too much for her to handle. She tried to remain at work but subsequent mistreatment by senior nursing staff and a physical threat by a male employee made it impossible for her to keep working. The hospital eventually admitted liability and Mandy was paid out. It goes without saying that she would have liked to work until retirement age.

The noise of the trams, the ever-increasing traffic and the closeness of the suburban houses had begun to grate on Mandy's nerves. She longed for peace and quiet and open spaces filled with birdsong and fresh air, so she persuaded her husband to consider moving away from the city. They settled on Greenmount and both loved it and wondered why they had not moved sooner. Their house was set on the side of a hill facing a mountain. There was a small stream on the edge of their property which flowed down from the mountain where Mandy saw platypus swimming occasionally and there was an abundance of birds and wildlife in the adjoining forest. It was paradise.

Mandy kept in touch with some of her friends from Melbourne but was keen to meet new people in Greenmount now that she had settled. The weekly meetings with the other newcomers seemed to be working out well; she had wondered if the age difference might cause a few hiccups but it had made no difference at all.

Her son George had worked in Berlin and London as a journalist for several years and to Mandy's delight was finally coming home for good. Her daughter Poppy was married and living in Sydney. Being separated from her children was difficult and she was hoping her daughter Poppy along with her husband would soon move back to Melbourne also.

She decided she would have a party for her next birthday which would coincide with George's return to Australia. She would invite all her new friends and families from Greenmount, her son, her daughter with her husband and children and Astrid's cousin Marjorie whom she had not met yet. This, she thought, would help to cement the new friendships.

16

Felicity

Felicity felt she was a failure. She had recently turned fifty, her two daughters who were both studying in Melbourne rarely came home and her husband, Jack, was always at work. Work had taken top priority in both their lives, with each of them working fulltime when the girls were little. Jack was now the principal of a large private school in nearby Kelvington and had no time for anything else. Felicity wondered what it was exactly that kept him there so late every day. She had her suspicions but did not have the energy to go there. Felicity had first trained as a kindergarten teacher and later studied to become a social worker thinking that was where she could do the most good. She had a big heart and good intentions but now she realised she had probably ignored the needs of her family in order to get where she was.

But, she thought to herself, where have I got to? I have no family to speak of and I am always embroiled in other people's problems. I am not even very good at my job any more because I'm always tired or hung over or, heaven forbid, depressed.

When she got home each evening the first thing she did was pour herself a glass of wine and the second thing she did was to turn off her phone. After two glasses of wine she would make herself something to eat then settle down to drink the remaining wine. Often she fell asleep on the couch and stayed there all night.

Most mornings she was woken by her husband who came into the kitchen to make coffee before going to work. He left a mug of coffee beside her, they grunted at each other and he disappeared through the front door.

This is not the way I wanted my life to be, she thought as she struggled to the bathroom. A hot shower woke her properly and only then could she turn on her phone. Upset to see the missed call from Mandy regarding Kathy sedating the children, she had quickly returned the call. When Mandy told her that Tommy had been admitted to hospital again and she had discovered the children were being sedated by Kathy, she somehow felt partly responsible. She felt she should have done more but as usual she was overloaded with work.

17

Kathy

Kathy was getting desperate. In her lucid moments she knew what she was doing was wrong but her need for Wayne and his presence overshadowed everything. Tommy's last admission to hospital had been very trying for her because she could tell that the staff members were beginning to be suspicious of her. They had questioned her repeatedly about Tommy's seizures and her life as well. They had other people present who took notes and looked at each other when she gave certain answers. In addition the nurses were monitoring Tommy more often than usual and to top it all off they had put him into a room right next to the nurse's station where they could see him through a large window at all times.

Tommy recovered and nothing abnormal was found so he was discharged again. This time a request was made to the District Nursing Service to pay a daily visit just to keep an eye on Tommy and his mother. A nurse visited only once because Kathy convinced her that they were okay. The nurse, who had a very busy schedule, was grateful because she had so many physically needy patients to visit that one less patient would make a big difference to her demanding day.

18

Café

The following week when Mandy and Astrid arrived at the café, Jane was not there and although they waited for her before ordering, she did not appear.

"Maybe she is sick," said Mandy, getting up and approaching the counter to order their coffee.

"I'll look out for her children at school pick-up today and ask them," Astrid replied. Quickly downing her coffee she looked at her watch and said, "It's time to go."

"I might as well come with you," replied Mandy.

When they reached the school there was no sign of Jane or her children but they did see Kathy's twins, Amy and Ruth, heading off towards home. Mandy said goodbye to Astrid and caught up with the two little girls, offering to walk home with them. On reaching Kathy's house the girls removed the front door key from under the mat and let themselves in.

"Where is your mummy?" asked Mandy.

"She is in hospital with Tommy again," said Ruth, beginning to cry.

"How long has she been gone?"

"Two days," Amy sobbed.

"Did the ambulance come again?"

"No, I think she took him in the car," wobbled Amy.

"We were asleep," said Ruth.

"It's okay, I will take care of you." Mandy bent down and gathered the two little girls into her arms to comfort them. As they helped Mandy to pack their clothes she gently coaxed them to talk about how their mother had left them this time.

"Did you take the pink medicine that Mummy mixes with ice-cream?"

"Yes, we have to take it or she'll put the pillow on us like she does to Tommy."

"What do you mean, she puts the pillow on you?"

"If we don't take the medicine, she says she will put the pillow on us like she does to Tommy."

"On your face?"

"Yes, and it makes Tommy sick and then she has to ring the ambulance."

Oh I see, Mandy thought to herself, so that's what caused the seizure—that is, if he even had a seizure. She took the two little girls hand in hand, one on each side of her, and walked back to the café where she collected her car and drove the girls back to her house. The more she thought about the children the angrier she became that this had happened again. This time it was worse because the girls had been on their own for two days! That was risking their lives as well as Tommy's. It was criminal, extremely dangerous and unforgivable.

Mandy fed the girls and settled them down to watch a video of Snow White while she made a phone call to St Mary's Hospital. This was the hospital where Mandy had worked and she had had no communication with anyone there since leaving and that was the way she had wanted it to stay. However this was too serious for her to hesitate over so she rang and was put through to the ward where Tommy and Kathy were. She spoke to the unit manager and explained her reason for calling. She left her phone number and received a call from the doctor ten minutes later.

The doctor was shocked by what she told him but at the same time he had suspected something of the sort, though not partial suffocation.

"I will get the Department and the police involved at once," he said.

"Can you give the children's father my phone number and ask him to ring me as soon as possible?" Mandy asked. "Oh, and tell him the girls are with me."

"Of course, and I will be in touch with you again soon, I will need to speak to you again in more detail. Thank you."

Mandy sank down onto the couch between Amy and Ruth, put an arm around each of them and they watched the remainder of the DVD together, the three of them laughing and singing along with the seven dwarfs. "Hi Ho, Hi Ho, it's off to work we go."

Wayne rang that night after speaking to the doctor. He was so upset he did not know what to say. However he did say that he would never have believed Kathy was capable of such dreadful treatment of their children and that he blamed himself for her breakdown and subsequent awful behaviour.

Mandy assured him the girls were alright at the moment but that he needed to come and see her so they could have a big talk in the next day or two.

Wayne picked up the girls from school the next day and brought them to Mandy. He looked dreadful and it was obvious he'd had a rough night.

"I have really messed things up," he said.

"Well not really, we will never know if Kathy was going to become so disturbed anyway," Mandy answered. "Something else in the future could have caused her to have the same or similar reaction."

"She did have a few strange quirks to her personality but I never thought it would come to this," Wayne said.

"Is she receiving psychological assessment?"

"Yes, and she'll lose custody of the children."

"Well, that's for the best, she could have killed one of them." Mandy shuddered inwardly at the thought.

"Oh god," groaned Wayne, shaking his head, "don't I know that; I can't stop thinking about what could have happened."

"Wayne, as much as I like your girls, I can only help you out short term—that is until you have worked out what you are going to do, but I can't care for them indefinitely."

"I know that Mandy, and I really appreciate your help. My mother is coming this weekend to look after Tommy and I will see what she is willing to do to help in the future. As you know Grace is about to give birth any day now so I can't expect her to look after three extra children yet, if ever."

"Well the girls are certainly welcome with me now and I think they will be happy here for a little bit longer."

Wayne bathed the girls after dinner and settled them in bed with a story and a few funny songs which made them laugh.

"I'll come and get you on Saturday and Granny Peggy will be with me. Won't that be nice?"

"Yes," said Amy. "But we like being with Mandy, she is like Granny Peggy."

"Yes she is like Granny Peggy and we are very lucky to have her," Wayne agreed.

The girls hugged their father and said good night. He blew them a kiss, turned out the light and left the room.

19

Marjorie

Astrid's cousin Marjorie had been about to turn sixty when her husband of thirty years unexpectedly left her for a much younger woman. This prompted her move to Greenmount where she taught in the local primary school for a number of years before taking early retirement. She was happy now that she was able to devote her time to her sewing, her garden, a dog, a cat, six chickens, a rooster and four geese, plus she enjoyed an occasional holiday interstate or overseas.

The idea of having Astrid and Julie living with her pleased her for two reasons; firstly because she was sometimes lonely for family contact and secondly because she had sensed Astrid was in need of a change in her life and Marjorie was able to help her achieve it. There had been an unexpected connection between them at the funeral of the elderly aunt whom both of them had loved. Astrid had not brought Julie with her to the funeral and Marjorie had said that she would love to meet her. "Why don't you come to my place for a weekend visit and then I can meet Julie?" Marjorie had suggested.

"I will; Julie would probably love to get out of the city for a few days and so would I." Julie never saw her grandparents and Marjorie had no grandchildren so there was an instant need fulfilled for the three of them.

A few months went by and after several visits by Astrid and Julie, Marjorie decided to ask them to come and live with her. It was an unexpected surprise for Astrid but she was extremely pleased and it didn't take her long to accept. She knew the close relationship she had with Marjorie could only be beneficial to herself, Julie and Marjorie. Astrid applied for a job at the Kelvington hospital and was offered three shifts a week, which was just what she wanted. She checked out the local school for Julie and resigned from her current job and in six weeks she had moved in with Marjorie in the verdant village of Greenmount.

Marjorie's two daughters were both working in the UK and were not planning to come home anytime soon. She had travelled to London to see Angela marry an Englishman and it seemed she might have to do the same for Bethany, who was engaged to a Scot in Edinburgh. She wanted them to come home and have their babies in Australia and make her a grandmother. The two girls kept telling her there was plenty of time and she kept telling them that as they were both nearly thirty, time could be running out. "That biological clock is ticking," she had said to both her daughters.

Marjorie's husband had left her for a younger woman over ten years ago and had died a year after. Marjorie wasn't sure of the circumstances of his death but she had her suspicions that it could have been over-exertion in the bedroom. She had been told he died in bed in the daytime and as he had always fancied himself as a bit of a stud she felt sure he had died with a smile on his face, and genuinely hoped so.

"If he'd stayed with me he would probably still be alive; I stopped enjoying and participating in sex years ago which I suppose is one of the reasons our marriage failed and he left me," she confessed to Astrid.

"Our marriage wasn't easy. He was a very good-looking man and women were always making themselves available to him. I knew he had a few affairs but I just got on with my own life and my own friends. It was the daughter of one of these friends who finally caused him to leave me and we divorced so that he could marry her. Unfortunately for them the marriage didn't last long because of his untimely death. I hope he was happy for that short time, I suppose he was if he had plenty of sex."

20

Jane

Jane was an attractive woman of above-average height with long, sleek dark hair and huge brown eyes. When she turned up at the café the following week looking anxious and a bit thinner, the others noticed that she did not look her usual well-groomed self. Once they had ordered their coffee and settled down for a chat, she apologised for not being there the previous week.

"I had an enormous shock, a life-changing shock," she said.

"What's happened?" Mandy asked.

"It's Rick, he has left me." Jane's eyes filled with tears.

"Oh no," Astrid said.

"Oh yes." Jane wiped her eyes. "I was shocked and I am very angry with him, but now that it's happened and I've had time to think I can see it's best for me and the children. I am very hurt considering what I did to try to keep our family together but I am determined not to fall in a heap like I did when he went to jail."

"Jail!" exclaimed Mandy. "Yes," replied Jane. "Three years ago he embezzled money from the company he co-owned."

"Oh Jane, you must have had an awfully hard time."

"Yes, and I've had enough. I am determined to put it all behind me."

"Why has he left you?"

"Same old thing," muttered Jane, "another woman, someone who I thought was a friend. Apparently it was going on for ages even before he went to jail."

"You didn't know?"

"No, not at all, I didn't have a clue. He tells me he still loves me and the children but he just can't stand to live the way we are now. He is very materialistic and vain, he likes to think people look up to him and admire him—even envy him—and no one envies him now."

"He says he still loves you, that's ridiculous," said one of the women. "Yes I really laughed at him when he said that. It's obvious our priorities are very different."

Jane went on to tell her friends that the day Rick left her he told her he had taken a day off work and was planning to go to the city by train. She drove the children to school and when she returned he was waiting for her to drive him to the station. As they pulled out of the driveway Rick asked her to stop because he had forgotten something and he ran back inside. He'd left his phone in the console of the car and it rang. She didn't answer it but looked at the screen and a text message appeared saying—

"See you at Southern Cross at 11am can't wait to see you, PIX. xx"

The message was from Pixie who along with her husband had been their best friends when they had lived in Brighton. When Rick came out through the front door he was shoving something into his jacket and Jane was sure it was his passport. Of course he denied it but with that and the text message it was obvious something was going on. When she pressed him for an explanation he said, "Drive me to the station please, I've left a letter for you under your pillow."

"I got out of the car and ran inside to find the letter. Apparently, he and Pixie had been having a casual affair for a long time (casual on his part) but Pixie always wanted him to leave so they could be together. He said she was crazy about him and when he contacted her with a proposition she jumped at the suggestion. She has pots of money from a big family company and she has bought a business for them in Tasmania that they intend to run together. And they're planning an overseas trip as well."

"You didn't drive him to the station did you?" asked Mandy.

"No I certainly did not. When I went back inside with the car keys I locked the door and the last time I saw him he was running down the hill towards the station." Jane sat silently for a few seconds then she said, "would you believe that just last week I thought I was pregnant and wondered if a new baby would help cement our marriage. Thankfully I am not pregnant because I would literally have been left holding the baby."

"Well," said Mandy, "I don't know how you allow these unwanted pregnancies to happen these days when you have so many choices of contraception now."

"Yes that's okay if the man remembers to buy condoms, which is what we were using," answered Jane, feeling a bit like she had just been told off.

Mandy let out a huge sigh. "You don't know how lucky you are. Until the sixties when the Pill became available we had very little contraception, it was often hit and miss. Condoms were only for sale in chemist shops but they didn't all stock them. Particularly if the business was owned by a Roman Catholic. And also the chemist would only sell them to adults, never teenagers."

"Really? Do you mean you couldn't buy them in the supermarket?"

"No—only some chemist shops sold them. I remember a friend of my brother's was dared by his mates to go to the local chemist and ask to buy condoms which he did, but the chemist refused to sell him any and rang his father to tell on the boy."

"What!" You're joking aren't you?" the group all reacted, astounded at the idea.

"No, it's true," said Mandy, "It was very different then and there were a lot of unplanned pregnancies, abortions, shotgun weddings and babies put up for adoption. It happened to many of my friends; I am so glad that's mostly behind us now. That's why I get annoyed when I hear about unplanned babies being aborted."

"You are right," said Jane, "I should never have trusted him. I could have been faced with having an abortion or not. I'm so glad I don't have to make that decision."

Astrid butted in to say, "As a nurse, I have heard some very strange stories from women regarding contraception. One old dear who had eight children and twenty grandchildren told me her only form of contraception was after sex to quickly get out of bed and 'sit on the potty and cough'. She had eight children so I don't suppose it worked very well."

"Oh that's beautiful," laughed Mandy. "We nurses all have stories to tell. Listen to this one. I met an elderly woman who had a very sad life and no children. We got talking and she said she would have loved to be a mother but her husband had not wanted any children so they only ever had anal sex. She said she was eighty and still a virgin, vaginally that is. The poor old dear, I think her husband, who was long dead by this time, was a cruel selfish bastard."

"She should have left him," said Jane.

"It was not easy for a woman in those days to leave but having no children I suppose she could have, but there was a stigma attached to a failed marriage so maybe she couldn't face the ridicule." Mandy answered. "Thank goodness times have changed and women on the whole are better off."

Jane listened to the stories the two nurses told about the sad women and was surprised to hear such things. "I'm amazed at the things you two have come up against: is that usual?"

"Yes. Nursing puts you in touch with anyone and everyone—you go into it young and innocent and come out with a very broad mind and amazing knowledge of the human race," Mandy said.

"I could write a book about people and the strange things they do. Another time perhaps," remarked Astrid.

Mandy turned to Jane and asked, "Jane now that you are single and NOT pregnant, what are you planning to do?"

"Well I do have a plan; it's something I have thought of previously and I just have to sell it, and I am going to start right here at this café."

"Sell what?"

"I am going to bake and sell good quality cakes and tarts suitable for serving in restaurants and cafés. I'm not a bad cook actually, and it's something I can do at home and deliver during school hours. I'll take a sample of various things that I have made and the café or restaurant can order according to what they like. I will be busy if it's a success but I can do it without upsetting the children's lives again."

"What a great idea. I have read about someone else doing just what you are proposing and it turned into a big business; I hope it succeeds," Astrid replied encouragingly.

"I don't want a big business, I want a small manageable one that will fit in with my family life and help me pay the bills," Jane said.

21

Rick

Rick was a selfish, arrogant man who knew he was giving up a good woman for not such a good one but he needed to have money and status and this was a quick, easy way to get it. He had not said that to Pixie, of course, when he got in touch with her: instead he told her that he had missed her and had her on his mind constantly. Pixie, who was still infatuated with him, fell for his lies and without much prompting suggested buying a business away from Melbourne where they could live and work together. Thrilled to hear from him and at the prospect of having him in her life again she jumped at the chance.

"Leave it with me," she told him eagerly. "I'll find something suitable."

She employed a broker who found her an eco-friendly tourist business on the east coast of Tasmania. It consisted of extremely luxurious cabins set on the side of a hill in semi-bushland overlooking the sea. There was a café on the property which she planned to turn into a fine-dining restaurant using locally sourced organic food.

From the time he first contacted Pixie until the day he left Jane it was only two months, and they had not previously seen each other for more than three years. As he travelled to the city on the train it occurred to him that Pixie might have lost her good looks or become overweight and that worried him until he saw her. He was pleased to see that Pixie was as attractive as ever. Looks were extremely important to him and he wanted a good-looking woman beside him. He smiled as he looked her up and down.

Smiling back at him she gushed, "Rick you look wonderful, I have been so looking forward to today, I can't wait for this new life together to begin."

They embraced and Rick said, "It's great to see you again Pixie."

Pixie was in seventh heaven, at last she had what she wanted.

A taxi took them to the airport and they flew to Tasmania that afternoon.

Pixie had arranged everything and there was a hire car waiting to drive them to their destination. She had visited the business before buying it and she chatted about how nice it was and what they could do to improve it, as they drove down the east coast of Tasmania.

Rick was impressed with what he saw when they arrived. It was much better than he had imagined. The cabins were well-insulated and had double-glazed windows and an air lock entrance which made them suitable for year-round use. They were up to date and luxuriously decorated and furnished and each had an open fireplace and a view of the bay. The property was planted with indigenous plants within the existing trees and shrubs and there was an abundance of beautiful birds and small animals in the area to add to the innate beauty of the place. Even the café was in good condition, though needed a bit of tweaking to get it to the standard of restaurant they had in mind.

The previous owners were only staying till the end of the week to show them the ropes so after putting their bags into their apartment, Rick and Pixie began working in their new business at once.

Their first night in bed together was wonderful, it was like the beginning of a new affair, full of sparks and passion but with the added advantage of knowing each other's bodies and remembering how to please each other.

"I hope that's an example of how we will be in the future," said Rick.

"I don't see why not," Pixie replied, snuggling into him.

Pixie was so happy to be with Rick at last and hoped that her plans would all fall into place. She was banking on him eventually running the business without her so she could resume her usual occupation of swanning around, looking beautiful and not doing much.

22

Pixie

Pixie, whose name was really Isabel, had been called Pixie for as long as she could remember. Her mother's pet name for her as a child was Pixie-bell because of the 'bel' in her name and because she looked like a little pixie. It was shortened to Pixie and it just became her forever name. She had enjoyed a privileged childhood as the only child of both doting parents and grandparents. Several generations of her family had owned a chain of hardware stores which they had sold for an enormous amount of money to an even bigger company. The money had been reinvested in real estate and they had gone from ownership of property to development of huge luxury apartment complexes. Pixie was very wealthy and because she had always got what she wanted as well as what she needed, it never occurred to her that she should not have everything her heart desired.

She had been quite happy with her husband James until she met Rick. She had become friends with Jane at the gym where they both worked out and as they got on so well together they eventually began socialising with their husbands and children. From the time Pixie first met Rick she wanted him badly, in fact she was so obsessed with him that she encouraged a friendship between the four of them. She invited

Jane, Rick and the two children to their home for a barbecue and then dinner and eventually organised for the two families to go away for a week in the snow. It was there that Pixie managed to get time alone with Rick and so started their affair.

Her husband James was totally unaware of the relationship until the night before she left him. She told him and then she told her two boys who just stared at her before walking off into their bedroom, tears falling silently onto their Lego pieces as they sat on the floor and tried to play. They were only ten and eight years old but had spent a lot of time without their mother, who had employed a nanny to help look after them. Fortunately they were fond of the nanny and she was fond of them.

James rang his mother who arrived the next day declaring that she was not surprised and had never really liked Pixie or trusted her anyway. Thankfully his mother was more than happy to step into the position of mother to the two little boys. Pixie had suggested that the boys could fly to Tasmania for the school holidays, otherwise she would come over to see them when she was able to. The boys needed mothering so badly they quickly allowed their grandmother to take over where Pixie had failed.

23

#

The day after Astrid visited her parents she received a phone call from her uncle.

"Astrid," he said. "You had better sit down, I have some bad news for you. Are you sitting down?"

"Yes," she lied.

"It's your father. I'm sorry to tell you, he's dead—he died yesterday afternoon. He fell from the balcony and your mother found him unconscious, barely alive. An ambulance was called and he was taken to hospital but died of severe head injuries a short time later."

"Oh," said Astrid.

"I know it must be a shock for you."

"Well … yes." Vision of her father as she had last seen him sitting in his wheelchair on the balcony flashed into her mind.

"Your mother is really upset, as you can imagine."

"Yes, SHE would be."

There was a long silence then her uncle said, "Is that all you can say?"

"Well I don't know what to say."

"Well, you could say you are sorry; he is my brother as well as your father that I'm talking about and he is dead. You were there yesterday weren't you?"

"Yes, I left about 1pm. Why?"

"Where was he when you last saw him?"

"On the balcony."

"That's where he fell from."

"Is that where Mum found him—below the balcony?"

"Yes, in the garden below the balcony; she said the railing was broken and that he must have fallen through."

"Okay, so he is dead. I'm not going to pretend to be sorry, because I'm not."

"Astrid, what are you saying, what do you mean, you're not sorry?"

"You know that he abused me, that's why I'm not sorry."

"Yes but that's in the past; you have to forget that."

"It's still fresh in my mind and it will never leave me that he ruined my life. I don't think you realise just how serious the sexual assault of a child is."

"Okay, but will you come to see your mother with me tomorrow to help sort out the funeral plans?"

"No. I saw her yesterday and that's more than enough for me. I don't like my parents and I don't care about the funeral plans."

"I can't believe your heartless attitude," her uncle said "Your mother needs you and your brother to help her through this."

"My mother's attitude to me and my brother was pretty heartless; we needed her to help us through our childhood and she did the opposite. Neither of us will help with the funeral arrangements or go to the funeral. Besides, I have to work an early shift tomorrow so I couldn't go with you even if I wanted to. Goodnight."

Astrid hung up, her heart racing. She felt light-headed and quickly sat down. She did not like confrontation at all because it always made her feel anxious.

Marjorie had overheard most of the conversation and was shocked at Astrid's attitude.

"Did I hear correctly that your father is dead?" Marjorie asked.

"Yes it seems he fell from the balcony yesterday after I left him."

"Aren't you upset?"

"Sort of, but I'm glad he's dead."

"What has made you so bitter towards him, Astrid?"

Astrid sat down, shaking uncontrollably.

"I'll make you a hot drink," Marjorie said. She returned with the hot tea to find Astrid head in hands, moaning and shaking.

"Astrid dear, what is it? Tell me," she said, putting her arms around her.

Astrid eventually calmed down enough to drink the tea and looked at Marjorie.

"I hate my parents. I have not told many people why I hate them but it's because of my father's abuse of me and my brother. It was dreadful and it went on for years and some of it was unbelievably cruel and degrading."

"Astrid, I had no idea."

"Most people had no idea."

"What about your mother?"

"Oh, she knew but she did nothing to prevent it."

"Really?"

"Yes. He preyed on me and he threatened me so that I wouldn't tell anyone."

Astrid sat upright and finished her tea. "Can we drink something a bit stronger?" she said to Marjorie.

Marjorie poured two glasses of brandy and handed one to Astrid. Astrid sipped her brandy and sat back in her chair. "It started when I was really little so it seemed like it was always a part of my life. He didn't actually have intercourse with me at first, that came later, but he did all sorts of degrading things to me or made me do things to him. I was confused because he told me I was special but I didn't feel special.

"He was cruel to my brother and turned him into a sad, nervous boy with no self-confidence then he would berate him for having no courage. When he tried to fight back, my father became violent with all of us, so we all adapted our behaviour so that we kept the peace."

"Astrid I am so sorry. If I had known I would have taken you both away from them. I always thought you were the perfect family."

"Everyone did, we put on a good show. We were pretending. It was the only way we could cope. Then one day he did one of the worst things ever. You will probably have trouble believing me but I swear it's true."

"Tell me," said Marjorie, her heart beating fast.

"He made my brother and I stand at the foot of his bed and watch he and my mother having sex."

"What! Really?"

"Yes, you heard, he made us watch them have sex, and we were so young."

"Oh my god, this is dreadful—the filthy bastard! I hate him too. Why would he have made you watch them?"

"I have no idea. Maybe it gave him a big thrill or maybe it was his attempt at sex education, I don't know."

"Oh Astrid, you poor dear girl."

"There are so many things I could tell you but I think I have said enough for now; it's too painful to bring it all up at once. I won't be able to sleep tonight."

"Will you go to the funeral?"

"No, and neither will my brother; we decided a long time ago not to go to either of their funerals."

"I won't be going either now that you have told me that," said

Marjorie. "Do you want me to inform other members of the family or do you want to keep it quiet?"

"I want people to know," said Astrid resolutely. "I want people to hate him."

Marjorie hugged Astrid and they both shed a few tears before going to bed.

Marjorie was up in the kitchen again at midnight because she couldn't sleep. She made herself a cup of tea and sat at the table shaking her head; she did not shed more tears, just sat engulfed in an awful feeling of despair and guilt.

"If only I had known, those poor little children," she kept saying, "If only I had known."

24

Mandy

Mandy received a phone call from the doctor she had spoken to about Tommy at St Mary's Hospital. He asked her if she could be present at a review of Tommy's case which was to take place at the hospital the following week. Mandy was not sure that she wanted to step inside the hospital but the doctor said there were a few people who would like to speak to her so she agreed. She was not keen because the last time she had walked out of the door she had been in a terrible state and had to be escorted out by the Human Resources manager. It held too many bad memories for her and there was a time when she couldn't even drive past the building without having an anxiety episode. However, she wanted to help Tommy so she told the doctor she would be there if she could bring a support person for herself. Felicity agreed to go with her.

They drove to the hospital together and on the way Felicity said that she would come into the meeting with Mandy but would have to leave early. She had an unexpected appointment at a nearby hospital and would come back for Mandy about 2pm. Mandy was a bit upset that Felicity was not able to stay with her, then told herself not to be silly, that she would be okay once she was in the meeting room.

The review was attended by various medical staff including a psychologist, the physician and the neurologist who had treated Tommy, a senior nurse from the ward, a play therapist, occupational therapist and a social worker, all of whom had been involved in Tommy's care. Each had their say and had pretty much all reached the same conclusion. Mandy was questioned about what she had discovered and it was noted that she was presently caring for Kathy's twin girls. At the end of the discussion and the presentation of results of tests and records of events, the summing up came to the conclusion that Tommy had no existing illness other than asthma and that his hospitalisation had been a result of his mother drugging him with Promethazine* (Phenergan) and partial suffocation by his mother placing a pillow over his face.

Kathy had been diagnosed with Munchhausen by Proxy**, also known as Fabricated or Induced Illness, a rare condition where a person makes another person in their care, usually a child, sick in an effort to gain attention for themselves. Kathy had been referred to a clinic where she was currently an inpatient undergoing treatment. The seriousness of Kathy's mistreatment of her child in order to gain attention was considered an extremely dangerous crime and the syndrome is recognised as child abuse, therefore Kathy had lost custody of the three children.

Mandy was commended for her alertness and reporting of her suspicions regarding Tommy's illness. They all agreed she probably saved his life or at least saved him from sustaining brain damage. The doctor thanked her for assistance and for being present today, shook her hand and left.

Mandy sat and waited an hour for a phone call from Felicity as

---

*Promethazine (Phenergan): an anti-histamine which is sometimes used as a sedative.
**Munchhausen Syndrome: a disorder in which those affected fake illness to draw attention to themselves. Munchhausen's by Proxy: where a carer, guardian or parent makes their charge sick in an attempt to gain attention for him or herself.

they had arranged. It was nearly three when she finally rang and asked Mandy to meet her at the front of the hospital at three-fifteen.

Mandy knew the hospital well so she took the quickest, most direct route to the exit, hoping not to bump into anyone she knew. As she walked down a corridor she admired some children's artwork which had been framed and hung along the walls at child's eye level. They were the usual pictures of houses, animals and rainbows, all innocent and charming. As she passed an open door she stopped to admire a pink unicorn running over a green hill as it reminded her of the pastel-coloured animals in Disney's Fantasia. To her left, from an open doorway she heard her name mentioned.

"That was Mandy Lewis who just walked by."

"Who is Mandy Lewis?"

"You know—she was the nurse who left after a patient died because of her negligence," the first voice said.

"I don't remember her."

"It was a few years ago."

"It must have been before my time."

"Well, I remember it very well because we worked together," the voice replied.

Mandy froze, mixed feelings of anger, fear and a need to flee came over her but she waited and took several deep breaths, allowing time for the rage and fear to subside a little, then summoned up the courage to walk back to the open door.

"Hello Cheryl, how are you?" she said in a loud voice.

Cheryl's face turned a deep red as she looked at her in surprise, "Oh, hello Mandy, I haven't seen you for a long time."

"No, well I left here quite a few years ago and have had no reason to return until today. Tell me, are you still living at the same address in Kensington?"

"Yes I am, why?"

"Because you will be receiving a letter from a solicitor shortly because of the defamatory comment you just made about me. It was not my negligence which caused the child's death and if you had bothered to keep in touch with me or even ask me about it at the time I would have been glad to tell you the full story. I was in need of support and got none from you or any of my colleagues. Actually I did get some advice from the unit manager, she told me to have a drink to calm my nerves and that was all.

"I was cleared of all responsibility and because of the pain and suffering and PTSD I endured I was paid by the hospital until retirement age. I hardly think that would have been the case if I had been to blame."

Leaving Cheryl silent and open-mouthed, Mandy turned and quickly headed for the door, the sunlight and the fresh air. She fell into Felicity's car feeling faint and began to shake uncontrollably.

"What's wrong Mandy?"

"Just what I feared would happen and worse."

"Mandy, I'm sorry I left you for so long, the doctor kept me waiting for ages."

"It was bad timing—I just happened to be there at the wrong time." She began to cry.

"Do you want me to stop?"

"No, keep going and don't stop until we get home."

Mandy kept her eyes on the familiar horizon. She could see the beautiful mountain ranges coming closer and closer as they sped towards home. Eventually she calmed down and was able to speak. Haltingly she told Felicity what had happened in the hospital after the meeting. She described the scene with Cheryl at the doorway and what she had overheard her ex-colleague say. She told her that she had once considered Cheryl a friend but that she was known as a gossip, often causing trouble with her big mouth. The accusation she had made about Mandy today was typical of her irresponsible behaviour and runaway comments.

They had an hour of driving ahead of them so Mandy decided to tell Felicity the whole story of what had caused her to leave her work at St Mary's Hospital some years before.

25

Mandy

"My work was in the paediatric ward at St Mary's and I will never forget the circumstances of that day and the days and months that followed. It began with a little girl who had been playing unsupervised with a lighted candle and sustained sixty-five percent burns when the flame ignited her clothing. She spent two days in the intensive care unit but was transferred to the ward mid-morning on the third day. The child's condition was not stable and she should have remained in intensive care but they needed the bed. I received a handover from another senior nurse who had been caring for her on the morning shift and we both agreed that the child was in need of a greater hourly rate of intravenous fluid as she was losing a large amount of tissue fluid through her burns. She and I agreed that she needed a review at once.

"The first thing I did when I took over her care at two-thirty was to contact the resident doctor who I knew, her name was Penny and she had been a member of the surgical team for about three months. I told her of my concerns but she did not come to see the child—instead she told me to continue with the current orders and take blood for analysis at six pm because that was what the consultant wanted. She was a very conscientious doctor but she often got flustered by the heavy workload and responsibility. Because of my concern I took the blood earlier, at five pm, knowing that the fluid imbalance would be reflected in the blood results. Meanwhile the child's urine output dropped below the minimum safe level and was like treacle and then her blood pressure dropped.

"I rang the registrar this time and he told me to stop measuring the urine so often. We always measured the urine output hourly for the very reason that it shows the state of hydration of a patient and any impairment in kidney function."

"How could you measure the urine so accurately?" asked Felicity.

"The child was catheterised," Mandy replied.

"About eight pm I received a phone call from the lab telling me the child's blood results were seriously out of balance and to ring the doctor at once. I rang the resident again and discussed the situation with another of my colleagues and we decided to contact the Registrar as well. He said he was busy and would speak to Penny at once. Penny arrived about nine-thirty and began looking at charts, making phone calls and writing new orders. I approached her asking if I could increase the intravenous fluid now but she lost her temper and told me to wait until she had spoken to the consultant, from whom she was expecting a call at any moment.

"When I finished the shift and left at ten pm, new orders had not been written, let alone started. I rang the next morning to ask about the child's condition and was told by one of my colleagues, 'She died overnight but we are not blaming anyone.' I was devastated and cried out of sadness and frustration.

"Two days later when I returned to work, no one mentioned the child. I asked if we were having debriefing and was told, 'we had that yesterday but we didn't ring you because we didn't think you would want to come in on your days off'.

"How wrong they were, I needed debriefing and understanding

from my colleagues but none was forthcoming. In fact I was lied to and given bad advice and wrong advice and as the days continued with no help, I became really depressed. When I finally had a so-called debriefing it was far too late, I was seriously injured. I was diagnosed with post-traumatic stress disorder and I was unable to work. All of this could have been avoided by two things—if the medical staff had heeded my warning and my manager had taken seriously my spoken need for debriefing following the child's death."

"What did the medical staff think was the cause of death?"

"There was some disagreement between them but ultimately it was shock leading to sepsis because of severe dehydration. Shock can be a serious condition which occurs following trauma and excessive bleeding and or fluid loss. There is insufficient blood volume to keep the internal organs working and they begin to fail, causing death unless there is medical intervention in the form of large volumes of fluid, blood or blood substitutes. That is what the child needed and did not get."

"Why?"

"Well, I was told on the night that the consultant did not want his orders changed without speaking to him first, and apparently he was not easy to contact.

"The whole thing is a tragedy from the initial burn right through to her death and beyond. I still think of this little girl every year on the anniversary of her death. I could have just given the child more intravenous fluid without the doctor's orders: no one would have been the wiser and I wish I had."

"Would that have made any difference?"

"Yes, I am sure it would have kept her going until the medical staff had got around to reviewing her," Mandy answered sadly.

"Oh dear."

"I had to take some time off due to anxiety and depression but when it was time to return to work on the ward I just couldn't do it. I was given another temporary position but people ignored me, even people who I had worked with and known for years. One woman even locked her office door at lunch time so that I could not speak to her. I had thought she was a friend. They just didn't want to know me.

"There were other incidents that really affected me and I lost heaps of weight because I couldn't eat or sleep, and I was jittery all the time. The people who shunned me—the people who I thought were my friends—were all working in the caring profession of nursing."

"It's unbelievable!" Felicity exclaimed.

"I know, but it's all true."

"When did you leave?"

"It was about twelve months after the child died. I was having a hard time getting used to the new job they gave me, it was rather demeaning but I was determined to keep working until something more suitable came up, and I did apply for a nursing position which didn't include much patient contact but the director of nursing wouldn't even look at my application. Then one day a young man who was under my employ threatened to harm me; in fact he said he wanted to hit my head against the wall and throw me down the stairs. That was the last straw for me, I just lost it. I threw my ID badge and pager onto the desk and said I couldn't take any more humiliation. I began to cry and I knew I had to go and I would never go back. I rang my son and asked him to come and get me. Someone from the HR department came and walked with me out of the hospital to where my son had come to pick me up, I couldn't drive I was so upset."

"What had you done to the guy who threatened you?"

"Nothing. I actually felt sorry for him because it was obvious he was a young person with problems and trying to find himself. I had offered to help him do some training to become some kind of medical technician which he said he wanted, but I think in retrospect he had other problems and he took it out on me. Perhaps he hated women, perhaps he had some bigger problem, I don't know. It was awful and I was badly affected by the whole thing. I stayed at home for ages, I couldn't go out on my own, I had trouble sleeping and I cried or lost my temper at the drop of a hat. I had bad dreams about the hospital and some of the very sick children I had cared for over the many years I worked there. The lack of support from my colleagues was very hard to take and I came to the conclusion that I was not liked. It took me more than a year to begin to turn the corner and I still have dreams about it to this day."

Mandy took a deep breath and said, "I will never get over it completely. I had better stop now, this is going to upset me for days and days, plus tomorrow I will have to speak to the solicitor who handled my case. I am going to ask him to send a letter to Cheryl because she is the type of person who says what she thinks without considering the consequences, often upsetting people, and she needs to be told."

"That was a terrible way for you to end your career," Felicity murmured.

"Yes it was awful, and other things happened to upset me more, but the worst thing was that no one seemed to care about the dead child except me and her parents and no one except my family really cared about me."

The remainder of the journey home was completed amid small talk or silence, each of the friends thinking over the day's events. Felicity had wanted to share the outcome of her appointment with Mandy but after what she had just heard she thought better of it.

When they reached Greenmount, Felicity reached out her hand to hold Mandy's and said, "I am really sorry about what happened today. I wish I had not kept you waiting for so long, but I couldn't get away any sooner. I am going to join you and Jane and Astrid next week and I will tell you about what I was doing today. Oh, and I might bring Eva with me, I think she will fit in with our little group."

"Thanks Felicity; I'm sorry I talked about myself and my problem all the way home and I didn't even ask about you."

"It's okay. I'll see you next week."

26

The following week the three women met as usual at the café they frequented. Seating themselves outside, it was difficult to hear each other as a large flock of sulphur-crested cockatoos screeched from nearby gum trees. Some of the birds hung upside down, showing off the pale yellow tinge under their pristine white wings. This week the friends were pleased to be joined by Felicity and Eva. Felicity introduced Eva, telling her that their weekly catch-ups were like group therapy and they each looked forward to seeing each other and letting off steam.

"It's group therapy with love," said Jane.

Eva said she was flattered to be invited to their group and told them she was on long-service leave and caring for her elderly mother, Martha. The women all welcomed her and asked if she was a cake sharer or did she like to eat a whole cake on her own.

"I like to share and get a taste of as many as possible," she answered. So instead of one cake between them they shared three of Jane's delicacies—a slice of citrus tart, a piece of flourless almond and pistachio cake, and a lemon friand. Everyone agreed the cakes were delicious and wanted to know how Jane's little business venture was going.

"Quite well so far, I have permanent orders from three places in Greenmount and another three in Kelvington," she smiled. "Several other places have shown interest and have said they will get back to me. I don't want to go too far afield because I have to deliver and that takes time," she said.

"Have you tried the restaurant in Forests-End? Their food is good but the desserts are always lacking," suggested Eva.

"Yes that's one of the places I'm waiting to hear from."

"John knows the owners there; I'll get him to give them a nudge," said Mandy.

"I didn't know about your business, Jane," said Felicity.

"Well I had to do something because now that Rick has left me, I want to be here for the children after school and weekends, not working away from home."

"I think that's a very good idea, and I'm about to do something new also," said Felicity.

"What do you mean?" Jane asked.

"I had a big scare with my health recently and although there is a positive outcome it has made me rethink my life."

"What was the health issue?" asked Mandy. "Do you want to tell us?"

"Yes—it was a breast lump which turned out to be a harmless cyst, not breast cancer. I already had myself dead and buried. Last week I went to see a specialist following an aspiration and biopsy and even though the results are good, I got a big scare and decided it was time to change a few things in my life. I've resigned from my job and will only be there until a replacement is found. I am going to live during the week with my two daughters in Melbourne and come home on the weekends to be with Jack."

"What does Jack think about that?"

"He doesn't seem to mind what I do. I don't think he cares actually, so if I am not here he might start to care."

"What about your girls—how do they feel about you moving into their house?"

"Well it's not actually their house, it's mine but they live in it and pay the utility bills. I think they are pleased. They are probably hoping I'll do a bit of home cooking—and I will—but I'm also going to do some work with homeless women and children with a charity called Help and Protect."

"Out of the frying pan into the fire, isn't it?" said Mandy.

"I'll only be working three days a week which will be a big change for me," Felicity answered. "I think I'll enjoy working part-time."

"Good luck with that Felicity, but that means we won't see you any more."

"Yes you will. I'm going to do some entertaining on the weekends when I'm at home so you will probably see more of me!"

There was something else at the back of her mind that she wanted to share but decided not to risk it. Some things were just too difficult for people to understand. Felicity felt she had almost made a fool of herself this week with her husband. She had suspected that he was always at work because of a woman. She was not sure which one it was but assumed it was his deputy, Sally Jones, who had been appointed last year and just happened to be a very attractive woman. Felicity thought it better to get it out in the open so she asked Jack about Sally's performance as deputy as an opener, giving him a chance to reveal their affair.

"It's funny that you should ask me that today of all days," he said.

"Funny why?"

"Well, it has not turned out to be a good decision to give her the position because she just can't do the job to the standard we require. She doesn't get things done on time and she is always taking days off, plus there is another problem that came right out of the blue."

"Oh?"

"She's been having an affair with another teacher on campus. The students have got wind of their relationship and are making things very tricky."

"Who is the lucky man?"

"There is no lucky man, Felicity, it's a woman. It's Diana Peters, the maths-science co-coordinator."

"Wow, that's a big surprise! I thought she was happily married."

"So did we all and we were all wrong."

"What are you going to do?"

"Well, I had a meeting with them today and they accused me of being homophobic, which I am not."

"No that's true, but isn't this bisexuality not homosexuality?"

"I don't know what it is, but I didn't think to tell them my own brother is gay and I'm okay with that.

"I told them that if they had kept the relationship quiet it would not have been an issue. They are not the first and they won't be the last couple to meet in a school, but they were seen standing very close together holding hands and gazing into each other's eyes by the students, who thought it was a big deal. Someone drew a cartoon of them and there are dozens of copies circulating around the school."

"What was the cartoon?"

"Very lurid—naked flesh, pubic hair, tongues, all that you would expect teenage boys to think of when they know two women are lovers."

"Have you got a copy?" Felicity joked.

"Yes, as a matter of fact I do." He reached into his briefcase and removed an A4-sized piece of paper which he handed to Felicity.

"Hmm, very well drawn, very good likeness. This student should be getting 'A' for art," Felicity smiled as she handed the cartoon back. "What was the outcome of the meeting?"

"They are both leaving of their own choice," Jack said, grim-faced.

"Well, I suppose that makes it easier for you except that you have to fill two positions."

"I have people I can promote for now, people who will do the jobs as well and, in the case of the deputy, better."

Felicity laughed to herself: boy did I get that wrong, she thought.

27

Kathy

Sadly Kathy did not respond well to treatment and it seemed as though she would remain an inpatient for a long time. Her parents were keen to take her home with them but she was far from well enough. She showed no interested in anything, just sat most of the time staring out of the window until someone came to take her for a meal or for a walk outside in the large gardens which surrounded the complex. Quite a few of the residents went outside and some even helped with the gardening, planting seedlings, raking leaves or pulling up weeds. Kathy didn't object; she went outside but once again she just sat and stared ahead, not interacting with anyone or anything. When the bell rang for lunch most of the residents hurried inside to eat but Kathy had to be taken by the hand and led to the dining room. She picked at her food and what she did not eat the others ate for her.

The occupational therapist encouraged her to try little projects but without any success. She took Kathy outside and pointed out the flowers in the garden, telling her their names. Beautiful rich red roses, the pink and white peonies or irises, but Kathy barely looked. She was given simple craft work to try but it remained on Kathy's table unfinished. A cat which had made itself at home in the garden shed gave birth to six dear little fluffy grey and white kittens and the occupational therapist put one of the kittens into Kathy's lap one day, but although she looked down at it she did not touch it, even though the kitten was mewing. Many of the other residents wanted to cuddle and play with the kittens all the time.

A psychiatrist visited her briefly every morning and tried to get her to talk but she remained silent. Then in the afternoons she was taken to group therapy where the other inpatients usually had something to say, but not Kathy.

A visit from Wayne drew no obvious reaction until after he left, when silent tears cascaded down her plump cheeks. One of the nurses observed Kathy standing at the window watching Wayne walk away and asked her why she was crying but Kathy did not reply.

Kathy's mind was foggy and her body was lethargic. She liked to sleep in and when she got up would sit in a chair and fix her eyes on something within her vision and stare and stare until the object became distorted. Sometimes a halo appeared around a head and she wondered if she was looking at an angel in heaven. Her thoughts were very muddled and the voices of the people around her sounded far off and obscure. She enjoyed being on her own in her own strange world where no one could intrude most of the time. On the few occasions that Wayne visited her she felt some disjointed sadness but had trouble understanding why.

The psychiatrist was not happy with Kathy's inactivity and lack of interaction and decided to change her medication. Kathy was not aware of the different medication but the staff began to see a slight improvement. In the past, the one thing Kathy had used as comfort was food but since being in hospital she had lost all interest in eating and had to be pushed to eat even the smallest amount. Someone sat with her at meal times encouraging her to eat a little food and drink something but the amounts were minuscule and she refused to eat more. The staff at the clinic supposed that she would be with them for months.

28

Wayne

Wayne's new partner, Grace, gave birth to a baby boy called Fin who was thriving and sleeping for long stretches, so Tommy was able to be at home with Grace, with whom he had bonded. Grace was very fond of little Tommy and very upset that he had been treated so badly by his mother. She was managing quite well with Fin and Tommy but Wayne worried that it was too much for her so soon after Fin's birth. He took as much time off work as he was able to help Grace so she could rest and bond with the baby. He insisted she stay in bed in the morning with the baby while he looked after Tommy, then when Grace got up to have a shower he carried the baby in a sling as he washed dishes or hung washing on the line.

Wayne and Grace decided to build a granny flat in their back garden for Granny Peggy to live in so that she could help with the children. But until the flat was built, Peggy and the children were to live in Kathy's house in Greenmount and the girls could remain at their school for the time being. Tommy would also be with Granny Peggy and the girls, leaving Grace to concentrate on baby Fin. To Wayne, who was trying to do the right thing for everyone, this seemed like the best solution. He discussed it with Grace who assured him she was happy to have Tommy with her, but he thought she was just being too cooperative and too nice.

The day Granny Peggy and the children were to move into Kathy's house in Greenmount was a Saturday. It was a long drive from the other side of Melbourne and Tommy fell asleep in the car. Wayne decided to take Granny Peggy and Tommy to the house before going to Mandy's to pick up Amy and Ruth. Tommy was lifted out of his car seat, put into his cot and tucked in without waking him. Wayne drove away to pick up the twins and Granny Peggy went to the kitchen to see what was in the pantry, thinking she would probably need to do some shopping for food when Wayne returned.

Wayne was only gone a few minutes, probably not even at the end of the street, when Tommy awoke and began to scream and yell out at the top of his voice. "No not be here, not be here, not be here…"

Peggy ran to him at once and picked him up out of the cot and carried him into the living room. "What is it darling boy, what's wrong?" said Granny Peggy as she tried to comfort him.

He continued to cry, "no not here, not be here, Daddy, Daddy, I want Daddy."

Peggy took him outside and sat on a garden seat under a large shady tree. Eventually Tommy began to calm down but continued to repeat again and again, "not be here, not be here".

When Wayne returned with the twins he was very upset to find that he had caused Tommy so much anguish.

"I should have thought about him being frightened of the house but it just didn't occur to me. He will have to come back with me and Grace. I should have listened to Grace, she wanted to keep him with her but I thought it would be better my way. This means the granny flat will have to be at the top of my list of things to do. I'll push for it to be built as soon as possible," Wayne said, almost in tears. "Oh my god, I've really stuffed up everything."

"We'll sort it out, but what about the girls, will they be okay here?" Peggy wondered out loud.

"Let's hope they are, otherwise we will have to rethink the whole plan," Wayne replied.

Wayne looked for the girls but they had already gone inside and were playing with their dolls' house. Wayne sat down on the floor with them as they began their game of making the perfect happy family in the dolls' house. Wayne watched them as they sat the mummy doll and the daddy doll together with the child dolls and mimicked adult voices reassuring them that they were loved and everything was wonderful. Wayne was amazed when he realised he was observing for the first time just how important it was to allow children to play to deal with life and its difficulties. He didn't want to interrupt them so he waited until the dolls were put to bed by a loving mother and father.

"Will you two be okay to stay here with Granny Peggy?" he asked."

"Yes," they both agreed, "then we can still see Mandy and John," said Amy.

"And we can go to our school too," Ruth added.

"Yes that's true, you will be able to go to your school and I will still pick you up on Fridays as usual and take you home to Grace and the baby, and when the granny flat is built we'll all live together again. Are you both happy with that?"

"Yes Daddy, we'll stay here with Granny Peggy. She reads us lots of stories and plays Snakes and Ladders with us and she lets us help with the cooking."

"You are such good girls and I am so lucky to have you. You know you can ring me anytime you want and I will ring you every night at bed time." He gave them a long hug and kissed them on both their cheeks.

"Good bye, I will see you on Friday," he said, standing up. Wayne left the room and said goodbye to his mother.

Tommy went back with his father and Grace was not at all surprised to see him. She did not say anything because she knew the whole thing was very difficult for Wayne and that he was trying very hard to do the right thing and keep everyone happy. She gave them both a hug and sat down to feed the baby while Wayne bathed Tommy and got him ready for bed. When she looked in the bedroom an hour later they were both asleep on Tommy's bed. Wayne was still holding a book, The Tale of Peter Rabbit, in his hand and Tommy was curled up under his other arm.

29

Jane

Jane's business was doing so much better than she had ever hoped. Word had got around and she was beginning to think she may have more orders than she could handle. She had to be very organised so she did the shopping first thing Monday morning after taking the children to school. To make things easier she began making enough pastry for the whole week on Monday afternoon and stored each batch individually in the fridge. On Tuesday morning she ground up biscuits for the cheese cake bases and made the citrus curd for the tarts and the cheese cake filling. On Wednesday, Thursday and Friday she made the flourless almond and pistachio cakes and assembled the tarts and cheese cakes as per orders. Most of the deliveries were done during school hours and sometimes after school with the children in the car.

Jane had always loved cooking and in her previous life she had been renowned at her dinner parties for putting on a meal worthy of one of Melbourne's top fine-dining restaurants. Her little enterprise was working very well and the restaurant in Forests-End had put in orders for cream brûlée which she delivered cold and the restaurant singed the top to serve. She was filling orders for six different places and it was just enough for her to handle on her own and to make a reasonable profit.

One day Jane was expecting a visit from Astrid and her cousin Marjorie who wanted to see how she made her delicious pastry. She had all the ingredients ready; the butter measured into 100g pieces, the flour measured and at hand and the egg yolks and water measured into 50ml lots. It was all done quickly in the food processor then wrapped individually in cling wrap and placed in the fridge till she needed it and it took no time at all in the food processor. She glanced up at the clock when the door bell rang. They are a bit early, she said to herself as she went to the door to greet the two women, but was surprised to see not Astrid and Marjorie but her estranged husband Rick.

"Rick—why are you here?"

"Hi sweetie," he said with a tentative smile. "I've come back."

"Back to Greenmount?"

"And you," he grinned at her.

"Not to me—you left me and our children to be with Pixie; what happened, didn't work out?"

"I made a mistake Jane, I realise now I should have stayed with you."

"Yes you should have, but it's too late now; it's over between us."

"Ah come on Jane, can't we give it one more go?"

"No, no, no we cannot. I had an awful time when you were in jail and I waited for you against my better judgment and my parents' advice. It was really difficult emotionally and financially. Since you have been gone this time, I've started a small business and I intend to keep it going. I have made some real friends here, unlike Pixie who I thought was a friend. The children are settled and I have enough money for day-to-day needs. I've realised I don't have to be rich like you do. I don't need the big showy house and flashy cars to make me happy; I am content with my life the way it is now."

This conversation took place at the front door and although Jane felt a little bit sorry for Rick, she did not want him to come into the house because she knew it would be difficult to get him out again.

Quickly she pulled the door closed behind her and put the car keys into her pocket and said, "Would you like me to drive you to the train station?"

"Come on Jane, don't be so difficult. Let me in."

"I am not being difficult, I'm being sensible; anyway I have plans for this afternoon."

As she said this a car driven by Astrid pulled into the driveway.

"Here are my friends to pick me up," she lied, "Goodbye Rick."

Jane opened the back door of Astrid's car and slid in. "Can you drive down the road—I'll tell you why as we go," Jane said to Astrid.

They drove to the shops and parked the car. Jane told them what had happened and as they were talking, they heard a train whistle as it was leaving the station. "He is probably on that train, it should be okay to go back now and I will show you how I make my pastry."

As they drove back Jane was hoping that was the last she would see of Rick for a long time. Every day it was becoming more apparent to her that he was certainly not the man she had thought he was when they had married.

As Astrid drove into the driveway Jane yelled, "my car has gone! He's taken my car."

"How could he? Haven't you got the keys?"

"Yes but he must have broken in and taken the spare key."

She jumped out of the car and ran around the back of the house and found the laundry window had been forced open.

"How could he do this to me? He knows I need the car and it's mine! My parents bought it for me."

"Well if he broke into your house and he stole your car he has committed two crimes, you have to ring the police," Astrid said.

"If I do he might go to jail again," said Jane.

"That's his fault; maybe he deserves to go back to jail. What about you, what are going to do without your car?"

"I can't manage the business without a car and I can't afford to buy another one at the moment, and I don't want to ask my parents for any more financial help ever again."

"So?"

"I suppose I have to ring the police. Do you know what is so silly?"

"What?"

"Well, you know my car, it stands out like a red flag—as you know it's a bright red Holden Cruse with personalised number plates. Jane-80. When Rick went to jail I had to sell my car but I kept the personalised number plates which he had bought for me with a new car as an anniversary present years ago."

Jane rang the local police station and gave the details of her stolen car to the sergeant who then put her on hold. When he returned to speak to her he was laughing as he told her, "We already have him on the side of the road. He was stopped for exceeding the speed limit."

"Oh dear, that makes three crimes," said Jane, "looks like he'll be back in jail again."

30

Pixie

Pixie and Rick had started off their new venture reasonably well because they were kept busy learning to run the business and hiring people to alter the café and make it into a good quality restaurant. Pixie planned to source local food where possible and needed a chef with imagination and modern flair. She had someone in mind who was working in Melbourne so she contacted him with an offer he could not refuse. The chef, Seb, travelled to Tasmania to see the place before deciding whether to take the position and found it difficult to refuse when he saw the surroundings and heard the added offer of very cheap accommodation for his wife and himself within the complex. Pixie was offering him free rein in the kitchen and he knew this was a great opportunity to make his mark and obtain the acclaim he desired. After spending a few days talking over the food available with Pixie, they settled on a menu putting a big emphasis on vegetarian and locally sourced food where possible. He knew that King Island to the north-west produced some of the best dairy products in Australia which would feature in many of the dishes. There were salmon and trout farms in Tasmania where they could always buy fresh fish. Seb also suggested they start a small kitchen garden even if it only produced herbs and greens for salads. He said his wife, who was a keen gardener, would probably be happy to look after the garden for them. He returned to Melbourne to resign from his present job with the intention of returning in a month to start work at the restaurant, which they had decided to call PIX.

When PIX opened, Seb and his menu were given wonderful reviews in the local newspapers and national food magazines. He and Pixie were spurred on and encouraged to keep up the quality and improve on it where possible. Rick, who was responsible for the wine cellar, loved playing the successful businessman and took on a bit of a pompous swagger which at first Pixie found amusing. He enjoyed telling people what to do and would not do anything that he thought was demeaning. Pixie sometimes had to help out with the cleaning if a staff member was sick or they needed to get a cabin ready a bit earlier than usual, but not Rick: he saw himself as a manager, not a worker.

Seb and Pixie started a kitchen garden at the back of the restaurant, growing herbs and greens and trying out various seedlings to see how they would grow. They erected a hothouse knowing the winter in Tasmania could be very cold. Rick didn't do any gardening, not even the watering, but he was full of suggestions.

Seb's wife Fiona arrived after six weeks and he cooked a special dinner to celebrate her arrival. It was from Fiona's arrival that Pixie noticed a change in Rick's behaviour towards her. He still wanted to have sex with her but it was just sex, with no affection or closeness; he seemed to have lost interest in her. The thing was, Rick had been struck by how much Fiona was like his wife Jane, the difference being Fiona was a flirt where Jane was not, and Fiona flirted outrageously with Rick, to his great pleasure and Pixie's annoyance.

Fiona was happy to become one of the staff doing anything that was needed, because she liked to be busy. Preparing the cabins, making beds, helping Seb in the kitchen or tending the garden; she just liked to have something useful to do. Pixie gave her the responsibility of checking the cabins and adding the finishing touches before occupation as they always had to be of a very high standard. This meant that Fiona often helped out with the last-minute cleaning and detailing. Strangely, Rick began offering his assistance at these busy times. Pixie thought nothing of it at first but twice Seb was looking for Fiona and twice she saw Fiona and Rick emerging from one of the cabins together and she began to get suspicious.

Pixie said nothing to Rick but decided to be vigilant a little longer because she hoped she was imagining things. One day when Seb was busy in the kitchen and Rick was helping Fiona with the cabins, Pixie decided it was time to investigate. When she reached the cabin they were in she found the door locked, which was unusual because it was common practice to leave the doors wide open while the cabins were being serviced. Also the curtains were all closed, that was unusual as well. Pixie went back to the office and picked up the master key for the cabins and quietly returned to the cabin and opened the door.

She was pretty sure that she would discover them in bed and that's exactly what she did find, except they were on the floor. At least they hadn't messed up the bed. They were in the throes of orgasm, totally unaware of her presence. Pixie stood and looked and in that moment she realised what a stupid thing she had done to believe Rick and to be taken in by his lies and greed. She did not say anything but turned and shut the door loudly so they would know they had been discovered.

Pixie returned to the office and rang her solicitor in Melbourne to tell him what had happened and ask his advice. He reminded her that the contract stated that in certain circumstances (and this was one of them) Rick would be instantly 'let go'. He was not an owner, he was an employee and as such could be fired because of unprofessional behaviour.

"Let me speak to him and I will explain the situation and the conditions," the solicitor offered.

Rick eventually returned to the office area and Pixie rang the solicitor again and handed the phone to Rick without saying a word. Rick had expected Pixie to make a scene and when she did not he was unsure what to think; maybe Pixie did not know about him and Fiona after all. Anyway he took the phone call and was shocked to be told to go at once and that he would be paid a small amount of money which he would be able to collect at a date to be arranged in Melbourne in person.

When he protested, the solicitor reminded him that he had signed the contract agreeing to those conditions and all he had to do was look at his copy to confirm it. In the meantime Pixie rang the police to have them on standby in case there was a problem.

Pixie went to the kitchen to speak to Seb who was obviously angry and upset with Fiona but not all that surprised. It was not the first time this had happened and he had had his suspicions.

"She is always misbehaving but this is the last straw," he said. "I told her the last time I can't go on with her but she just doesn't get it, she can't help herself."

If the police had not been on the premises Seb would probably have confronted Rick and punched him but he knew if he started something he would probably regret it, so he just told Fiona to get out of his sight. "You deserve each other," were his parting words to her.

Pixie was angry and upset with herself to realise she had been fooled by this shallow man but she kept her composure as she said to Rick, "If this had worked out between us I was going to hand the business over to you but you blew it big time. You are on your own again. I don't want to see you ever again."

She turned away from him, fighting back stinging tears of regret and disappointment, tears that she refused to let him see.

Rick and Fiona left with their tails between their legs. Seb and Pixie had made sure their car keys were in their pockets just in case one of the disgraced couple had plans to take a car. They had to stay in a local guest house overnight and hired a car to drive to the airport the next day. When they arrived in Melbourne, Rick contacted the solicitor and arranged an appointment to receive his payout. The amount he received was much less than he expected but when shown the contract he had signed, inappropriate behaviour and unfaithfulness were definitely stated as reasons for instant dismissal and the amount he was to receive was what he had agreed to. He would not be paid the money at once but in a week's time. When Fiona heard the small amount of money he was to be paid she was annoyed and decided to give Rick the flick, and headed back to her old stamping ground in Brunswick. Fiona had thought Rick was an equal partner in the business worth several million dollars and therefore she imagined she would be on easy street and it would be worth sticking around, but now that she knew the true situation she was not going to waste her precious time with him.

Fiona was a user of people as was Rick, and he had received a little of his own medicine and did not like it at all. True to form he thought of Jane and how he could use her for a while, so that was why he took a train to Greenmount that day and stole her car.

He ended up in jail again thinking over his recent mistakes, and he was angry with himself and everyone else. He did not give a moment's thought to the three women whose lives he had disrupted; he thought only about what he would do next for himself.

31

Pixie

Pixie had learned a very hard lesson and she was deeply ashamed of herself. She hated to think what people would say about her and was determined to somehow atone for her mistake, at the same time not wanting to give up on the business. Seb was also keen to stay as he, like Pixie, was enjoying the success of the restaurant, the lifestyle and the climate on the east coast of Tasmania. Pixie had kept in touch with her husband James and had visited him and the boys a few times in Melbourne. She thought of them now and decided after a few days of consideration to ring James with a proposition.

James heard her out and, surprised at what she proposed, said he would give it a few days thought and get back to her.

"At least he didn't reject my offer outright," she said to Seb.

Pixie's proposal to James was that as the business was doing really well, she thought it would make a wonderful venture for one or both of their two boys to take up and run when they were old enough. She and James could continue to expand and improve the property and business until the boys completed their education and then it would be theirs. "If things don't work out we can sell it."

The following week James contacted Pixie and said, "I have given it a lot of thought but first I have to come and see the place with the boys and my mother. Mum sold her house and has been living with us since you left and the boys have became very attached to her and she to them. The family now includes my mother as long as she wants to be with us; I can't disrupt her life again."

Pixie agreed but she dreaded having to live so close to her mother-in-law, who she knew had never liked her much and now probably hated her.

"Oh well, if that's what you want to do I will be happy with that," Pixie replied.

"Pixie, what do you have in mind for us as a couple—do you expect me to just forgive and forget what you did?" asked James.

Pixie was tentative in her reply. "I'm willing to try if you want to, but I know it will be difficult for you. Can we at least talk about it when you get here and give it a try?" she said.

"Okay," James said, "I'll see you in a week, and I want you to arrange for me to visit the school the boys would be going to: if the school is not up to scratch we can't come, we will have to stay in Melbourne. I will never send them to boarding school after what they have been through, it would destroy them."

When James and his mother arrived with the boys they were all impressed with the complex and instantly warmed to the whole idea, but James remained pragmatic and stuck to his requirements for the boys, their school, his mother, he and Pixie, in that order.

The school was small but very up to date and well equipped, and the teachers were old enough to have some teaching experience behind them but not so old that they had lost their imagination. They seemed motivated and happy to answer any questions James put to them. The boys, who were both keen on playing sport, were very pleased because they had a soccer team and swimming and sailing for school sports.

There was another staff cabin available on the complex where

James's mother could live which she liked very much as it had a nice view of the sea and there was a small area where she could plant her own tiny garden.

Then there was the problem of the relationship between Pixie and James, which would probably prove to be the most difficult thing of all. They set aside some time on their own when they could talk without interruption.

"What do you think?" asked Pixie, getting straight to the point.

"Pixie I still love you but I am still very hurt by what you did. However I am willing to give it a go mainly because of the boys. I'll take the long service leave which is due to me and at the end of that I will either stay or go, it all depends on what transpires between now and then."

Pixie was so relieved to hear what James had said that she had tears in her eyes as she replied, "Thank you James. That's more than I expected and so much more than I deserve. I promise I will do my best to make it work and I will try to make it up to you."

32

Kathy

At last Kathy began to show some improvement. One morning without being told she got out of bed, took a shower and went to the dining room for breakfast, surprising everyone. At group therapy that week she actually whispered her name and from that day forward there was a slow but obvious improvement. The thing that had prompted this amazing change, apart from the changed medication, was that for the first time in ages she had looked at herself in the mirror and was amazed to see the woman looking back at her; it was someone she hardly recognised, a face from the past, a slimmer, pretty Kathy; Kathy as she used to be. She turned in front of the mirror and looked at her backside and it was quite a normal size again and her hips were also considerably smaller. She was so astonished it gave her quite a jolt and she actually felt awake and alert for the first time in months.

The staff at the clinic were thrilled because they felt that their therapy had worked and they were congratulating each other for their ability and perseverance. Whatever the reason or reasons for Kathy's improvement, it continued over the next few weeks until she was finally let out on day leave with her parents. Following that it was overnight leave and eventually she was completely discharged from the clinic and attended weekly appointments with the psychiatrist.

Kathy's parents had not touched her old room but kept it the same as it had been before she had married. On entering the bedroom, she looked around at her bits and pieces still where she had left them years before. A pink teddy to hold her pyjamas was sitting on the bed, her favourite books in her bookcase, the same pretty curtains hanging at the window and on a shelf was a photo of herself and Wayne at a school social. Kathy looked at the photo and turned to her mother and said, "Wayne."

"Yes darling, that's Wayne."

Kathy did not mention Wayne again or ask anything about the children but when their names were mentioned she frowned and shook her head or shrugged her shoulders. The matter of her seeing them was brought up and it was hoped that in the future she could begin chaperoned visits. Kathy's parents saw the children sometimes but once they had Kathy at home with them it was difficult.

After a few weeks of living with her parents she began taking a walk in the morning just in the immediate neighbourhood. Each day she went a little bit further, sometimes stopping to look at places which she found familiar. Without knowing why she decided to walk up a hill to a white house with green shutters. She stood looking at it for some time before it came back to her this was a house she knew well. She went home saying nothing to her parents about the white house with the green shutters but she thought about it all that day and the next. Kathy knew the house was important to her and connected to Wayne somehow but as she was confused about what had happened over the last few years and not quite sure what the connection was or what had happened to her boyfriend Wayne or where he was, she decided to try to find him.

On the third day of approaching the white house with the green shutters Kathy walked up the garden path and stood looking at the front door for five minutes and was surprised when a complete stranger opened the door.

"Hello, can I help you?" said a young woman.

"Is Wayne here?" Kathy asked.

"Wayne does not live here," replied the woman.

"Oh. Where did he go?"

"The woman who used to live here has moved into an apartment in the city I think, so I suppose that's where Wayne is, but I'm not really sure and I don't have the new address."

The woman looked at Kathy's sad face and added, "I am sorry I can't help you dear."

"Oh," said Kathy, and she turned and walked away. Without returning to her parent's home she got on a train without a ticket and went into the city intending to look for Wayne.

33

Wayne

Wayne was a good tradesman with plenty of contacts in the building trade. Quite a few of these men owed him favours so he was able to call on a builder and an electrician to help get the granny flat built quickly. It was not a separate dwelling but joined to the house via the laundry. Granny Peggy was thrilled with her new abode and chose the decor to suit herself for the first time in her life. It had two small bedrooms, one for her with an en-suite and the other made entirely for the children to play in, with a sofa bed in case one of them slept over. There was a large living room, dining area and kitchen, perfect for a mature woman to live in alone.

The official move was on a Saturday and when the children arrived at the house they were overjoyed to find a black Labrador puppy waiting for them.

The children ran and the puppy ran after them yapping and nipping, trying to catch their feet. They threw a ball for the puppy to fetch and tore round and round the garden until they all got thoroughly exhausted.

"What's the puppy's name?" asked Amy.

"She doesn't have a name yet," said Wayne. "You can decide on a name between you."

"Let's call her Beauty," said Amy.

"Or Black Beauty," said Ruth.

"Blacky," said Tommy.

"Let's sleep on it we can talk about all those names and decide tomorrow," said Wayne.

The puppy woke up and after devouring a bowl of food began to play again, jumping and licking and yapping until it was exhausted and fell asleep on the kitchen floor. Wayne picked it up and put it in its basket and the children all gathered around to admire the beautiful sleeping animal.

"Looks like Sleeping Beauty to me," said Amy.

Grace and Wayne cooked a big dinner to celebrate them all being together at last. They sat down to eat as one big family and Wayne proposed a toast to their future together and the children all joined in clinking their glasses, saying cheers and clapping. Little Tommy cheered the loudest and it woke baby Fin and then he was the loudest. Everyone was happy. The children played with their dolls' house after their bath and went to sleep in their new beds in their new home after a bedtime story and a few of Wayne's funny songs.

Grace was sitting in the lounge room feeding Fin while Wayne put the children to bed. "Come and sit down with me Wayne. You've had such a busy time over the last few months. Let's hope you can relax a bit from now on."

Wayne sat down next to Grace. "Gee I hope so. I'm exhausted. I feel like I've earned a break."

"You have earned a break. Maybe you could take a week off work," Grace replied.

"Yes I hope so too but I've promised Kathy's parents that I will see them next week and arrange a regular time for them to see the children," he replied with a sigh. "We might have to wait a bit longer to have some time away."

"What about Kathy? When will she be seeing the children?" asked Grace.

"I don't know what the plan is for that," he replied. "It's not going to be easy though, particularly for Tommy. And the girls have stopped asking about their mother."

Wayne, trying to do the right thing for everyone as usual, intended to keep in touch with Mandy because the children loved her and John and they had helped him enormously with the girls, and they had all become very fond of each other. Mandy was also determined to keep in touch with them and mentioned that she intended to have a birthday party for herself soon and hoped to see them all on that day.

34

Astrid

Mandy began to plan her party. She felt it was a bit unusual to plan a big party for her own birthday but in reality it was more than herself she wanted to celebrate. It was a lot of things and quite a few people whom she thought deserved celebration. She had made friends with some wonderful people and their children and felt a party to bring them all together would help to cement the friendships even further. Astrid's cousin Marjorie, who was closer to Mandy's age, had become a friend, as had Wayne's mother Peggy, who had brought Amy and Ruth to see her at least once a week when she had been living in Kathy's house in Greenmount caring for the twin girls.

Eva kept in touch with Mandy and often met up with her and the extended group of women for a coffee and a chat when she had someone to keep an eye on Martha.

When Mandy made a list of people she wanted to invite she was surprised at how many there were. Well over twenty with the children. Then she began on the list of food she would serve. She decided on a healthy meal with lots of quality salads, fresh breads and cheeses, followed by enormous fruit platters and a cake. One evening as Mandy stood on the back stairs looking outside she pictured it all in her head:

a large marquee in the garden full of happy people chatting together, music playing, birds singing, children laughing and running up and down the garden paths. Unfortunately as she turned to go back inside she tripped going up the stairs and broke her ankle, making it necessary to postpone the party.

In the meantime, her son George arrived home from London and was living with Mandy and John while deciding what he would do with his life next. George had originally planned to be away for a few months but had ended up staying for three years. He fell in love with London and the English countryside and the easy travel opportunities to Europe. Most of the time he worked for a publishing company and it was in the office that he met Jennifer. They seemed to be well suited and had a great time together but as she was an only child of elderly parents she would not consider leaving them to come to Australia even for a holiday, let alone to live. George had always been very honest with Jennifer, telling her early in their relationship of his intention to return home to Australia, so when that time came they were at an impasse. They decided the only way forward was for them to separate. Sadly George returned home leaving an unhappy Jennifer behind.

After Mandy broke her ankle, instead of just meeting for coffee the group of friends often went to Mandy's house on Saturday afternoons to share a bottle of wine and to try out Jane's latest culinary delicacies. On one particular Saturday Jane arrived first with a smoked salmon and brie tart and was extremely surprised when the door was opened by a very attractive young man. Mandy introduced her to George, her son. He was on his way out, as Mandy explained later to the others, to meet up with an old girlfriend he had been out with several times since his return to Australia.

"I was hoping he would take a liking to either Jane or you, Astrid."

"Not me," said Astrid, "I don't want another man in my life ever."

"What—really not ever?" asked Mandy.

"No, not ever."

"What has made you so against men?" asked Jane.

Astrid looked at her cousin Marjorie for support for a minute then blurted out, "I was sexually abused by two men in my family and it's had a big impact on my life and my attitude towards men."

"That's dreadful, you poor girl," said Mandy.

The others agreed and were expressing their sympathy when the doorbell rang and Felicity arrived with another bottle of wine and a plate of savouries.

Felicity looked different, her wild red hair had been tamed and was now plaited and beaded and she was wearing a very colourful long dress in the style some African women wore. She looked happy and relaxed and different, and obviously content with her new self.

"Felicity you look wonderful," said Jane, "and so different."

"Yes," she said, "no longer the professional but a free spirit now."

She looked around at the others and said, "Have I interrupted something?"

"No not really," said Astrid.

"Well yes, actually, something very awful Astrid was sharing with us about her childhood," said Mandy.

"Oh and I barged in at the wrong time, sorry," said Felicity looking at Astrid. "Do you want to continue?"

Astrid looked out of the window to where her daughter Julie was playing with Jane's son and daughter and thought, compared to these happy children, how different her childhood had been and how she had suffered and said, "Yes I will."

She repeated all that she had told the others previously, stopping now and then to regain her composure. It was a harrowing tale to hear and they all had tears in their eyes as Astrid continued to speak. Mandy and Marjorie sat either side of her with arms around her shoulders to give comfort and support and were both visibly upset.

When Astrid stopped speaking they were all quiet for a while and then Felicity asked, "Is your father still alive?"

"No he died recently. Actually I killed him."

There was silence in the room for a few seconds and then Marjorie said, "What are you saying? You didn't kill him, it was an accident. He was on his own and fell over the balcony after you left him."

''Yes that's true but I set up the so-called accident hoping that it would happen and it did, and I am glad he is dead. I hated him and I hate my mother because she didn't protect my brother or me from the vile monster."

"What did you do to make your father fall?" asked Marjorie.

Astrid's voice was shaking as she replied, "Well it's a bit of a story. I was angry with him because he and my mother insisted that I visit them because they had something important to discuss with me. I didn't want to go but I was coerced into going by my interfering uncle. What they wanted was to have a relationship with their granddaughter Julie in return for me getting their money. I was absolutely furious and when I refused and mentioned his abuse of me, he laughed and said it was in the past and it was nothing, I was just a child and I should just forget it." Astrid stopped and took a few deep breaths.

"Are you okay to continue? You don't have to if it's too difficult," said Mandy.

"I want to get it off my chest and now that I've started I'll keep going. I was so enraged that he laughed at me I felt like kicking him but I kicked at the wheelchair instead. I missed, and my foot connected with the railing of the balcony and damaged it. The timber splintered and some pieces fell to the ground. He was really annoyed and he asked me to move him closer so that he could pull it back into place. I was going to just walk off and leave him but I suddenly thought of him tumbling over the edge of the balcony. When I moved him closer to the railing I didn't put on the wheelchair brake, thinking that if he leaned forward it would cause the chair to move towards the edge, hit the railing and perhaps he would fall over. Apparently that's what happened. I had fantasised about killing him many times but never had the courage or opportunity until that perfect occasion. I am amazed that he trusted me, that just shows you what an arrogant bastard he was."

Astrid finished talking and reached a shaking hand for her glass of wine. "I feel better now that I have that off my chest." She drained the glass and poured herself another. She did feel relieved to verbalise the events of that day but at the same time it became very real and now that other people knew, who knew what would happen to her. Thinking of Julie she wondered if she should have kept the event on the balcony to herself.

"Oh my god, that is horrific what you endured. It's a wonder you didn't kill him sooner," said Felicity.

"As I said, I'd thought of it often."

"What about your mother?" someone asked "Why did she put up with it?"

"That's a whole other story. She had a difficult childhood but I still can't forgive her for not protecting us," Astrid replied.

She didn't want to say anything else, she felt drained and leaned back in her chair closing her eyes. After downing her third glass of wine she fell asleep on the couch.

Jane went home with her children and Marjorie went home with Julie.

"I can come back for Astrid later," said Marjorie.

"It's okay, I'll wait a while and bring her home when she wakes," Felicity said.

Astrid awoke an hour later and apologised to Mandy and Felicity for going to sleep. "Has everyone gone home? They must think I'm very rude."

"No one thinks you're rude, we are all deeply sorry for what happened to you and we all want to help you in any way we can," Felicity reassured her. "I for one will never say a word to anyone about the circumstances of your father falling over the balcony, and each of the others said the same thing. We all agreed that what was said in this room today stays in this room."

"That goes for me too," said Mandy. "You have suffered more than enough and there is no need to bring up your father's accident again. It was an accident."

Felicity drove Astrid home later but they stayed in the car talking for an hour more. "I suppose you have had counselling?" asked Felicity.

"Yes, plenty of that but I have never told anyone, not even the psychologist, the end of the story or how the abuse ended."

"Why?"

"Because it was so terrible. I just couldn't think about it let alone talk about it for a long time."

"Do you want to tell me? I don't want to push you but if it will help to tell someone I will keep it a secret."

Astrid looked out of the window and took her time before beginning.

"When I was about fourteen my brother and I decided we couldn't put up with our parents' cruelty any longer. We decided to run away but we didn't get far because my father rang a district policeman he knew who picked us up at the local train station and took us back home to our parents, where we were yelled at and belted. My father said we had brought disgrace on the family. We couldn't fight back, we were overpowered by him, plus he locked us in my brother's bedroom without food for the whole weekend. My bedroom didn't have a door, remember."

"My father's disgusting abuse continued until I was fifteen when

I became pregnant. I didn't know I was pregnant but my mother was obviously more alert than I was, and because she did the washing she knew when I had my period. I knew about pregnancy but I could not link the awful abuse I was subjected to with the idea of a baby—I just couldn't see it as anything other than punishment for being a bad girl. They were always telling us we were bad children, specially me. Anyway one day my mother asked me to wee into a little jar and she took me to the doctor. When we went into the doctor's consulting room she handed the jar to him without a word. When he came back he nodded to her and said 'shall we proceed with the plan we discussed on the phone?'

"She said yes, but the words pregnant or abortion were never uttered in my presence. A few days later I was admitted to hospital as a day patient and had a termination without anyone ever consulting me.

"When I woke up from the anaesthetic a young nurse sat with me and held my hand. She must have assumed I had a boyfriend because she talked to me about various methods of contraception and that it was the responsibility of both people in the relationship. That, coupled with the fact that I was bleeding as if I had a period, made me assume the worst. I asked the nurse if I had been pregnant and she said to me, 'You didn't know?' I said nothing to her but she said she would look into it, but I never heard anything from her. Before I went home the doctor asked my mother if they should put me on the pill. She told him it would not be necessary. As we drove home the only thing she said to me was, 'You know you are a filthy slut don't you.'

"I went to my room and cried myself to sleep. Since that day nothing about the hospital or the termination was ever mentioned by any of us but my father never touched me again, thank god. I mean thank goodness, because if there was a god I am sure he would not allow such things to be done to innocent children."

Felicity was silent for a while and then she said, "I agree with you about the god thing, so many children have had to put up with awful things in their lives, there is so much evil and I refuse to call it a sickness, it's just outright evil and so many of the perpetrators just like your father get away with it. I wish there really was a god and hell where they could burn for eternity."

"Yes I agree. Thank you Felicity for listening to me, it's an awful story and I wish I could forget it but I can't, it pops up in my dreams all the time."

"No wonder," said Felicity as she took Astrid's hand. "I mean what I said Astrid, I will do anything that I can to help you. Ring me any time you need to talk."

Felicity got out of the driver's seat and gave Astrid a big hug before returning to the car and driving home to her husband Jack. She was not sure if it was her new look or her absence during the week that had caused him to pay more attention to her but whatever it was, they were getting on together better than before. She looked forward to closing the front door behind her and sitting in the quiet safety and comfort of their home, hoping it would help to ease the pain of the horrific story she had just heard.

35

Mandy

Mandy continued to hobble around and eventually had a moon boot fitted and hoped to soon be mobile enough to have her party. She was sitting with her leg elevated on a stool reading when her son George brought her a cup of tea saying he wanted to ask her about Jane.

"Tell me Mum, what is Jane's situation—is she single?"

"Yes she is single and has the two children you've seen with her."

"Does she have a man in her life?"

"No, I'm pretty sure she has had no man since her husband left her."

"Gosh, why would you leave a woman like Jane?" asked George.

"It's a long story, why don't you ask her out and maybe she will tell you all about it," replied his mother.

"I was getting around to that next; would you look after her children if I took her out for dinner?"

"Of course I will. I was hoping you would like her. She is a very good woman, strong and faithful and a good mother. I don't think you can get better than her. But what about your old girlfriend?"

"We are just old friends and that's all, nothing else—that was all over for us long before I went overseas. We've been out together lately because she has recently separated from her husband and needed a shoulder to cry on. We went out for dinner a few times. I think she wanted to make her husband jealous—which she did and now they are talking about getting back together."

"Oh, so you have served your time with her, have you?"

"Yes, but she has listened to me and helped me too. I told her about how difficult it was leaving Jennifer and how she wouldn't consider even a temporary move to Australia."

"Have you heard from Jennifer since you have been home?"

"Frequently. She wants me to go back but I have decided to put that relationship behind me as we had both agreed when I was still in London."

"I suppose she is heartbroken now that you have gone. Sometimes people don't realise how much they love someone until they are apart."

"Yeah well that may be, but now that I have met Jane it has helped me to get over Jennifer, even though I was very fond of her. Maybe I didn't love her after all."

"I'm sorry for Jennifer but I'm glad to hear that you are interested in Jane because I would love to have her in our family. She would make you a lovely wife and a great daughter-in-law for me and your father, and the children are really lovely."

"Mum! I'm thinking about taking her out for dinner, that's all."

"Well one thing leads to another... I'll just keep my fingers crossed; no harm in that, is there?"

"Okay, but don't hold your breath, she might say no."

George was fairly confident that Jane was a little bit interested in him as they had exchanged several secret smiles and glances at each other. They had bumped into each other in the local bank but she had been called into an office for a meeting with the bank manager just as they had begun to talk. He could have asked her to join him for a coffee but due to circumstances he didn't wait around. Later he was really annoyed with himself for being so silly, deciding to get her phone number from his mother following a little bit of information gathering.

36

Jane was not really surprised to receive a phone call from George and happily said yes to dinner. She had liked George from their very first meeting. She was happy and excited because she had not been out on a date for years and was thrilled to be asked. They decided to go out the following Saturday night and Mandy offered to look after Jane's two children.

Jane had a wardrobe full of extremely good clothes left over from her previous life and took some time choosing what to wear. Many of the clothes were too dressy for a semi-rural restaurant but she wanted to dress up and look her best. She decided on a slimline sleeveless black dress which she wore with one of her many strings of matching pearls and earrings. Freshly shampooed and blow waved, her hair fell onto her shoulders and framed her pretty face. Looking in the mirror she turned from left to right and was pleased with the way she looked, and it gave her a little unexpected frisson of sexual delight. She knew she looked her best and hoped George would find her attractive.

Mandy was so keen to help this relationship along that she picked up the children early so she and John could take them to see a movie and then out for pizza, giving the young couple plenty of time together.

George did a double take when Jane appeared at the door because, in spite of already admiring the way she looked, he had not realised just how beautiful she was.

"You look wonderful Jane."

"Thanks George; you look pretty good yourself."

"Have you eaten at the restaurant in Forests-End?" he asked.

"No but I do supply them with several of my desserts."

They spent a really enjoyable evening together and as the evening progressed George wondered again why any man would let this woman go. She was intelligent, educated and feminine. They discovered they both had a love of reading and enjoyed many of the same authors. Jane told George all about her cooking business and he was keen to try one of her desserts which were on the menu.

"What do you recommend?"

"Do you like creme brûlée?"

"It's one of my favourite desserts."

"That's my recommendation," she replied.

George ordered a creme brûlée and as he cracked his spoon through the firm toffee surface he said, "Can we do this again next weekend?"

Jane nodded and smiled at him, "I would love to."

George realised after his first date with Jane that she was not just any woman; to him she was already special. A woman worth knowing, worth wooing, maybe even worth marrying. He decided to take it slowly and he knew he would have to get to know her children because if they did not like him it was no use continuing the relationship.

George was smart enough to know that his mother knew quite a bit about all sorts of things due in part simply to the fact that she had been around longer than he had. She also knew a bit about children and she was very observant, something he never would have admitted as a teenager when he had thought he knew everything. But now older and wiser, he decided to speak to his mother and get her valuable advice. It wouldn't hurt, whatever she said.

They were sitting in the kitchen on Sunday morning sharing a pot of freshly brewed coffee when George said, "Mum, I really like Jane and I think I could very easily fall in love with her."

Mandy smiled broadly. "Great, that's wonderful," she said.

"Yes it's great, but there are the children and therein lies the problem. I need to get to know them and they need to get to know me. I can't become more involved with her if the children don't like me."

"I'm glad you are thinking of them George, but I don't think you will have any problems, just be yourself. Don't try too hard but at the same time make a little effort."

"I thought I would take them to the zoo, take a picnic, what do you think?"

"Look, I think that's fine, but simple things like just talking and listening to them, playing games or reading and talking about books you liked as a child... Maybe you could lend them some of those books, they are still in the bookcase."

"Okay—and also movies that I liked, most children like a good movie don't they?"

"Well you certainly did. And you could play a game of soccer or cricket with them."

"Good idea Mum. I knew you would have something useful to suggest."

"It's common sense my son, good old common sense," said Mandy happily.

George looked in the bookcase and found his old Tintin books which he had loved as a boy and had read over and over again. His sister Poppy had loved Tintin as well and they had both also loved the Roald Dahl story books, so he took them all. He hoped that William and Zoe would be happy with his choices.

Jane was pleased to see that George was making an effort with her children because she wanted them to have a good man in their lives.

They hardly ever saw their own father and he was not a good example anyway.

They had a great day at the zoo. Jane took a picnic lunch and they ate sitting watching a new baby elephant playing in the water. The children loved the orangutans which performed for them in a very cheeky way, making faces at them then sticking their bottoms against the glass so the four of them couldn't stop laughing.

On the way home the children both fell asleep in the back of the car, giving George an opportunity to ask Jane very quietly, "Do you think we could go away for weekend? Or at least one night?"

Jane put her hand on his and replied, "I'm sure we can manage one night."

The next weekend George picked Jane up before lunch and they drove to a charming retro hotel near Treetham. After checking in they put on sunscreen, donned a sun hat each and went for a bush walk. Map in hand they went looking for a waterfall where they could eat the lunch provided by the hotel. They sat in the shade watching the water cascading down the rocks, splashing at the bottom into a stream where a few children and their parents were wading in the shallow water. It was a wine-growing area so they also visited two wineries where they sampled far too much wine. Both of them were feeling happy and relaxed and just a little bit tipsy when they returned to the hotel later in the afternoon.

"I'm a bit intoxicated," said Jane grinning at George. "Too much wine and sun."

George had thought they would have a romantic dinner and then go to bed for the first time but when he asked Jane if she wanted to have a shower first, she replied, "I will have first shower if you have the first shower with me."

George laughed, "I was trying not to push you."

"We have done enough courting for now, I think we can take it to the next level, but George I really appreciate that you have been so considerate."

Jane pulled her t-shirt over her head and kicked off her shorts and was about to enter the shower when George grabbed her hand and pulled her to him.

They had kissed before but nothing else and never unclothed. As Jane went to him she undid the buttons of his shirt and pulled it off and he stepped out of his shorts. As they kissed their bare skin touched for the first time and there was a wonderful simultaneous rush of desire from them both. George lowered his head to kiss her neck and lick her nipples, Jane sighed and caressed his firm chest, running her hand across the hair and down his toned, lightly tanned body around to his bottom and pulled him close to her. A low moan escaped from George as he picked her up, kissed her again and placed her on the bed. Looking down at her body he said, "Jane you are so beautiful."

"Come here," she said, "I want you so much. I want to feel you inside me now."

George groaned and lowered himself over her. She wrapped her arms and legs around him and sighed with ecstasy as he entered her.

An open fire was alight in the restaurant which was softly lit and their table was just far enough away from the other diners to give them the privacy they wanted. The waiter was discreet and they enjoyed a delicious dinner flirting, kissing and whispering in the romantic atmosphere. As the evening progressed they were both well aware of the sexual tension which had developed between them during the past few weeks and since the afternoon it had reached a new height. George put his hand on Jane's thigh as they gazed into each other's eyes and both were excited and aroused at the thought of the night ahead where they could repeat their passionate lovemaking, perhaps more slowly this time.

37

Felicity

As Felicity walked to work at HAP in the morning it was one of the busiest times of day with people hurrying to their workplaces all over the city of Melbourne. She always carried small change in her pocket so that she could buy coffee and a bun for anyone she met who looked like they had spent the night on the street and might be in need of some breakfast. Although she offered help to these people she did not push too hard, assuring them that there was help available nearby if they required it. Some took her up on the offer but surprisingly others preferred to remain on the street, hoping to collect donations from strangers during the day.

Felicity enjoyed her work in the city at HAP because she found there was a real need for non-judgmental people to help with the very basic needs of homeless people. Her previous experience and contacts were invaluable as she helped the unfortunate people she came across. A large number of those in trouble were women who had managed to escape domestic violence inflicted by their husbands or partners or sometimes other family members.

She discovered there were a small number of women living in cars who had very little money for petrol. If they parked their car in the one place for too long they were asked to move and it was difficult to find a safe place, particularly if they had children. If a drunk man banged on the window asking for sex or just to terrorise the women, they were scared for their children's safety.

There were women who came to the shelter in only the clothes they were standing up in after fleeing a beating or rape by their husbands or partners. Sometimes they were assaulted on the street and their possessions were stolen. A few very unlucky people who had been very unwell and unable to work for an extended period became homeless because of loss of income. No work, no pay, and with no money to pay rent they found themselves on the street homeless. Not everyone had a caring family to fall back on

There were young girls who had escaped sexual abuse at home from mum's latest boyfriend or their own father or other family members, even brothers. It was pretty confronting at times but Felicity really felt it was work well worth doing and she really wanted to help as long as there was a need.

As the women came from all walks of life Felicity often said to herself, 'Heaven forbid, this could happen to one of my own.' Or thought of the paraphrased bible quotation her mother had been fond of: 'There but for the grace of god go I.'

38

Kathy

When Kathy reached the city she was disoriented and wondered where on earth she had come to, and why? As she wandered the streets she remembered she was looking for Wayne but she couldn't see him anywhere as there were so many people, so many faces, all different, all the same, rushing here and rushing there. As the day went by she became hungry and thirsty. She watched people eating at an outside café and when they had finished she hurried over and ate the leftovers and drained the drinks that remained in the cups and glasses.

She eventually found her way back to the train station but had no ticket so she was not permitted to enter. She didn't really know where to go anyway. Her mind was groggy and she was in a daze. As it became dark she continued to wander aimlessly until she saw a few people bedding down for the night so she sat near them.

An observant homeless woman named Jo had her eye on Kathy and could see she was not street smart and possibly in trouble. She watched her from a safe distance wondering if she should get involved; she knew a confused attractive blonde woman wandering around on her own could easily become prey to some opportunistic creep. As the night went on and there were more intoxicated men walking around the streets, she made a decision to help when she saw her being hassled by a group of drunks who looked like they were out on the town. Probably a bucks night, she thought; poor bride.

Jo approached Kathy and said, "Hello there lovie, do you have somewhere to sleep tonight?"

"No, I am looking for Wayne."

"Who is Wayne?"

"He is my boyfriend."

Jo could see that Kathy was confused and asked, "do you take tablets every day?"

"Yes."

"Have you taken them today?"

Kathy shrugged her shoulders.

"You come with Jo, my lovie, come with me and I'll find you somewhere safe and tomorrow I'll help you find Wayne."

Kathy didn't seem to notice Jo's untidy, creased clothing or her long untidy hair, it was nothing to her and in her compliant state she did as she was told. Jo took Kathy to her own sleeping place under a bridge that crossed the Yarra River. There she shared the space with about a dozen other homeless people most nights.

"Another lost soul, Jo," said one of the men, "You're an angel in disguise."

Jo provided Kathy with a fairly clean piece of cardboard to lie on and a grubby blanket with which to cover herself. Kathy didn't notice the grubbiness and, exhausted, fell asleep quickly.

Early next morning when Kathy woke, Jo had already been out and collected a few dollars from people on their way to work and bought two cups of coffee and a bun to share with Kathy. After eating, Jo took Kathy to a public convenience where she could use the toilet and wash her face and hands.

"Today we will try to find Wayne," said Jo.

It was mid-morning and Kathy's mind was blurry; she had missed three doses of her medication now and it was beginning to affect her more and more. Jo took her on a long walk up the top of a hill to the outskirts of the city to a shelter and charity run mostly by volunteers. As they approached the entrance the aroma of home cooking wafted out into the street,

"You'll get a good healthy lunch here," said Jo. Kathy was silent and stood still, staring into space. Although she was hungry, her confusion prevented her from thinking about food or Wayne. She wasn't really thinking about anything.

"Hello Jo," said a woman at the door, "we haven't seen you for a while, how are you?"

"I'm okay Janet but this one here is in need of some help, she doesn't know if she's Arthur or Martha."

"Come in and have some lunch and we will see what we can do to help her," Janet answered kindly.

Kathy and Jo were both given a bowl of steaming hot vegetable soup and a fresh bread roll each while Janet went to consult a social worker.

The social worker who was working that day happened to be Felicity who emerged from the office and saw a familiar face sitting and staring at a bowl of soup on the table in front of her. Not sure who it was at first she said, "I know that woman, I know her face but I can't remember where from."

She went over to speak to Kathy but Kathy just looked back blankly at her. Then Felicity remembered and realised who it was. She had heard that Kathy had lost a lot of weight but she also heard that she was in a clinic receiving treatment. Had she escaped, or been discharged on her own? That was not likely. She spoke to Kathy, "Hello Kathy, I am Felicity, do you remember me from Greenmount?"

Kathy shook her head and continued to look at her blankly.

"Come on love, you need to eat," said Jo, putting a spoonful of soup almost into Kathy's mouth. "You need this." Kathy began to slowly eat the soup herself.

It was not difficult to find Kathy's parents as she had been reported to the police as missing the day before. Jo stayed with Kathy as they waited for her parents, who arrived promptly with Kathy's medication and whisked her off home.

"Thank you, Jo, that was very kind of you to help Kathy. Can we help you with somewhere safer to live?" Janet asked her.

"No thanks," she replied. "As I've told you before, I'm okay and I feel a lot safer with my mates on the street than I ever did with the old bastard I was married to for twenty years. With him I was bashed and raped on a regular basis—hasn't happened to me once out there on the street, so no thanks, not now anyway."

"Well we are always here for you if you want us," said Janet.

"Thanks," she said again as she hurried away down the hill.

39

Felicity

Felicity could not wait to tell her friends about poor Kathy so she called in to see Astrid on her way home from Melbourne on Friday night. Astrid was upset to hear that Kathy had ended up wandering around in the city looking for Wayne.

"I feel so sorry for the unfortunate woman and her terrible situation. What will happen to her now?" Astrid asked.

"I'm not sure, maybe she will go back into the clinic for a while. That was an obvious setback," Felicity answered.

"The poor thing, will she ever be able to see her children again?"

"I hope so, but it certainly won't be soon."

"The big question is, will the children want to see her?"

"Probably," guessed Felicity. "Children usually do want to be in touch with their mothers even when they have been abused by them."

Astrid poured a glass of wine for them both and they settled down for a big chat. Two glasses of wine were always enough to get loose lips talking and today Felicity really wanted to get something off her chest.

"Astrid, you shared a big secret with me and because of that I wonder if I could share one of mine with you?" she asked.

"Yes of course you can," responded Astrid immediately, "and I promise to keep it a secret if that's what you want. You know I can keep secrets as I did keep mine for so long."

"Well, you remember when we first met at the shire office and I told you about the young woman who took her own life after having a stillbirth?"

"Yes I remember it well, a very sad tale."

"It was not exactly as I told you. It was a bit different actually. I told you nobody knew about her discharge from hospital but someone did know."

"Oh," said Astrid, waiting for Felicity to continue.

"Yes, I knew."

"You?"

"Yes, me. I received a phone call from the maternity hospital telling me about her and I took the details down and lost them. I don't know if I threw out a piece of paper or deleted a message from my phone because I can't remember how I took down the information. Whatever happened to the details it doesn't matter, because I never went to see her and I should have, and if I had she might still be alive today. I should have contacted the maternity hospital to get the details again but I was so busy at the time I kept putting it off and then, tragically, it was too late. I was sick with grief after her death and became depressed and started to drink excessively to deaden the guilt I was feeling. I will never forgive myself, not ever, not in a million years. I dream about her regularly and just can't get her out of my mind."

"Oh Felicity, I can imagine how you must feel but she might still have killed herself no matter what you or anyone else said or did. We know losing a baby and postnatal depression are very serious."

"I know that, but she did kill herself and we will never know what might have been. I have tried to make up for it in other ways but I can't, it's too big and too hard."

"You are always helping people and now you are doing something new and it seems you're doing a good job there, helping people who are in hopeless situations. I know how difficult it can be trying to juggle all the things people want you to do at once, far too much for one person to handle, and more requests and phone calls coming from all directions. My work is like that sometimes. Both you and I have to concentrate on moving on."

"Thank you Astrid, I can only try."

40

Eva and Martha

Eva continued her long-service leave and was able to care for her mother, Martha, as she had promised to do. It was an interesting time for Eva because she and her mother had never been close. Martha had always seemed to favour her two sons. The sons rarely visited their mother now and at last Martha began to see that Eva was a good daughter and even told people how glad she was to have a daughter like Eva. That was something she had never heard her mother say before and it surprised and pleased her.

The reason they had never been close was because Martha was very old-fashioned, even Victorian, in her attitudes, due to her upbringing by a strict father who was an old-fashioned Methodist minister. Eva was fond of saying what no one else would say and was often outspoken in her political and religious views which really annoyed her mother. Sometimes she had said too much and it ruffled feathers, quite the opposite to her mother who would do anything to keep the peace. They were mother and daughter but they were very different people.

When Eva was a young teenager and began receiving attention from boys and wanting to go out with her girlfriends, Martha did not approve and began to overreact to her daughter's budding sexuality. As Eva went through puberty her mother found it difficult to cope with her little girl growing into a pretty teenager and she began to panic. Sometimes they argued about silly things, like how long Eva's nails were or her hair being in her eyes and looking untidy or her slacks being too tight. Once Eva had got the sewing machine out and taken in her tartan slacks without her mother knowing. Martha took the slacks and cut them up for dusters.

Eva went to an all girls' school and when she was about fourteen her school had an annual social night with the local boys' school and of course she wanted to go. One day after an argument Martha said, "you can only go if you let me cut your awful long fingernails, they look like cats claws."

Eva argued with her mother but in the end agreed to a manicure because she really wanted to go to the school social. Eva sat on a kitchen chair expecting her mother to shorten her fingernails but Martha picked up the scissors and instead of picking up Eva's hand to cut her nails, she grabbed Eva's hair and hacked off a long tress.

"What are you doing! Why have you cut my hair?" screamed Eva.

"It needs cutting."

"No," Eva yelled as her mother cut the other side to even it up. "How could you do that to me? Now I'm ugly! No one will look at me. I hate you, I hate you! What have you done to me!"

Eva's auburn hair had been envied and admired by her friends at school. It framed her pretty face and matched the colour of her huge eyes. She loved her hair and always kept it clean and brushed. When she looked in the mirror and saw what she looked like she was distraught. Her hair was short and uneven, it looked dreadful.

Martha knew she had gone too far and regretted the impulsive thing she had done as soon as the first tress hit the floor. Eva became so distressed and made so much noise that Mrs Roberts who lived next door came and knocked on the door thinking something terrible had happened to them. She saw Eva's tearstained face and went away shaking her head in bewilderment. Eva went to school the next day and cried in the arms of a sympathetic teacher.

Eva went to the school dance and met her first boyfriend and kissed him, so even with her hair cut short her mother couldn't stop her daughter from becoming an attractive young teenager who appealed to the opposite sex. If Martha had known all about what happened in that first relationship she would have been horrified.

Martha's elderly father, who thought a woman's hair was her crowning glory, was angry with Martha for allowing Eva to cut her hair so short. He berated Martha and she swallowed his words in silence. No one told him the full story.

Now that Martha was an old woman the tables were turned and Martha sometimes behaved like a child, frequently calling Eva 'Mum' because she was so well cared for and confused at times. She rarely had to ask for anything because Eva knew her mother well. She knew what she liked to eat for breakfast and how many cups of coffee she had before lunch time, what television shows she liked to watch, the types of books she would read and how she wanted her hair done.

One day out of the blue Martha said, "Eva I have wanted to say something to you for years and years but I have kept putting it off."

"What is it Mum?"

"Do you remember when I cut your hair when you were about fourteen?"

Eva raised her eyebrows, "I'll never forget it," she replied quietly, remembering vividly that awful night and the subsequent days when her mother had taken her to a hairdresser to try to repair the damage she had inflicted on her only daughter.

"Well, I have never forgotten it either and I am so sorry that I did that to you, it was unforgivable. I don't know what came over me and I have regretted it ever since."

"I didn't like it much, that's for sure," said Eva remembering the sight of her hair lying on the black and green lino of the kitchen floor.

"It was a silly thing to do, I must have been mad," Martha said.

"Yeah, well I hated you for doing that to me but you weren't mad, you were naive and really silly sometimes. You didn't seem equipped to have a daughter like me although I was just a normal child."

Eva thought it better to say very little about the event and how it had affected her. She was over it now but had never forgotten how awful it had been. She knew Martha had expected her to be the way she had been as a girl, never questioning her parents and always doing as she was told. Eva had worked out that for some reason Martha was terrified of her daughter's evolving sexuality and had wanted her to remain a little girl.

"Yes I think you are right, but I was scared that you might get into trouble like my sister did, and look how she was forced to get married to that dreadful man and then had all those children. She had a terrible life, always pregnant and downtrodden."

"Fortunately I think things turned out pretty well for me, don't you think?" Eva asked.

Although Eva said that things had gone well for her it was not quite true. In the late sixties when the contraceptive pill became available Eva had a serious boyfriend and became sexually active. Sensibly she took the pill to avoid an unwanted pregnancy as many women were able to do at last. Eva had never been sure how her mother found out about her taking the pill but she did and she was ridiculously upset. Martha went to bed and cried and wouldn't get up for the whole weekend, then she went away to her sister Betty's place for two weeks to have a break and get over the shock of her 'promiscuous' daughter's behaviour. Before she went she made Eva feel guilty and she made her promise to stop taking the pill and stop having sex. Eva stopped taking the pill, that was easy, but abstaining from sex was just too hard. Martha being away for two weeks did not help as Eva and her boyfriend were alone in the house fairly often.

When Martha returned home she told Eva that Betty and her husband Bert thought taking the pill was a very sensible thing to do and much better than Eva having an unplanned baby when she was so young. Martha did not tell Eva it was okay to take the pill but it was too late anyway, Eva was already pregnant. She had a very regular cycle and as soon as she missed a period she suspected she was pregnant and the following week she developed morning sickness, confirming it.

Martha saw Eva looking pale and sickly emerging from the toilet two mornings in a row and said to her, "Eva, are you pregnant?"

"No I've got a virus. My friend Carole has it too. I have a headache and I think I have a temperature," she answered with false bravado.

There was no way Eva could tell her mother about the pregnancy after the way she had behaved when finding out about her taking the pill. She didn't want to be pregnant because it would prove her mother was right, she was not ready to have a baby, she was still a student nurse and too young. There had been several other student nurses who had left to get married for this very reason and she did not want to be one of them. Mostly, she did not want her mother to be proved right.

Fortunately she had a friend who knew someone who had had an abortion. Abortion was still illegal in the 1960s and the only way a woman could have a safe abortion was to go to a secret place and pay lots of money. Some women who couldn't afford a safe abortion either tried to end the pregnancy themselves or resorted to a 'back street' abortionist. It was not uncommon for women in these circumstances to get an infection due to an incomplete removal of the foetus, or severe bleeding which meant an emergency trip to a hospital. Some poor women became sterile and others even died. Fortunately there were also some doctors who would perform the procedure secretly but properly, and it was to one of these doctors that Eva went.

She arrived at the doctor's office at nine on the appointed day. She had not eaten breakfast because she assumed she would be having a general anaesthetic which the nurse had forgotten to tell her about. Putting $200 under the pillow as she had been instructed, she lay down and waited for the doctor to arrive. When he did enter the room he was wearing a white cap and a surgical mask so all Eva could see were his large brown eyes. He nodded at her and said good morning, nothing else. Without any explanation Eva's legs were put into stirrups and the procedure, the abortion, began. No anaesthetic and no explanation, no words of comfort, no hand holding, nothing, just the cold metal speculum inserted and opened wide in her vagina and then the dilators passing through her cervix one by one, opening it up to a size appropriate to remove the foetus. It was painful and degrading and when it was over she heard the foetus being flushed away down the toilet. It was not until later that night at her friend's place that she really thought about what she had done and that it was a baby, her baby, that she had heard being flushed away. It was an awful memory and one which Eva tried to avoid.

Martha continued to live happily with her daughter and son-in-law, enjoying the comfort of home and occasional visits from her grandchildren at weekends. Eva wheeled her on to the back veranda on warm days where she could doze in the dappled shade as magpies warbled and blue wrens flitted around the garden. Eva waved to her mother from the vegetable patch as she was weeding or planting in the garden.

Martha developed dementia and often said or did strange things. "I'm one hundred years old, aren't I?" she asked Eva one day.

"No, not quite," Eva answered, smiling.

"Well I know I am getting very old and I probably won't be here much longer."

"Yes, you are getting old but you are in good health; I think you will be with us for a long time yet," Eva replied.

"That may be, but can I see my baby Ruby before I go please?"

"Who is Ruby?" asked Eva."

"You know, that little baby of mine."

"I don't know anything about a baby called Ruby, I wouldn't know where to look for her," said Eva, slightly amused.

"She must be somewhere."

"Maybe under a cabbage leaf," added Eva with amusement.

"No that's where they come from, not where they go," Martha said.

Eva did not have an answer to this because she had never heard of a baby called Ruby, and as her mother did have a touch of dementia, she let it go.

Martha had led a healthy life but she was old and eventually became unwell. She awoke one morning with a very high temperature and a slight cough. She did not improve over the next twenty-four hours so Eva called the doctor who diagnosed bronchitis. Martha began a course of antibiotics which didn't seem to help much and her condition deteriorated rapidly.

Eva called the doctor again and they discussed admitting her to hospital. Martha was still eating and drinking a little but was short of breath and very sleepy. Eva did not want to send her mother to hospital even though she now had pneumonia and Eva could see she was failing fast. Medical intervention might only prolong her life for a short time and if she was going to die she would be more comfortable at home in her own bed. The doctor agreed and between them they decided to leave her at home on the antibiotics and paracetamol. Two days later, just after Martha had been washed and settled down to have a nap, Eva went outside to pick fresh flowers for her mother's room but when she returned, Martha had slipped into unconsciousness and died soon after, very quietly, in her own bed in her daughter's arms.

After the funeral Eva was given a recording of the funeral service so one day when she was on her own she went to bed and listened to the recording and thought about her dear mother Martha's difficult life and their difficult relationship. She cried as she had never cried before and then slept for several hours. When she woke she felt some relief from the strain of the last week leading up to Martha's death and the funeral.

The next day Eva decided to begin sorting out Martha's bits and pieces. Her mother had a beautiful old mahogany box full of letters and documents including a copy of her will, death certificates and marriage certificates. Eva began to sift through the old pages and came across love letters between her mother and father.

She read them, feeling a little like she was prying, but was also happy to read that they had been very much in love. In the box her mother had kept all sorts of things including baby teeth, tiny baby booties, hospital ID cards from when she had given birth to her babies and a lock of hair from each of them. Inside a large yellowed envelope she found a separate lock of hair which was tied with a faded pink ribbon. Scribbled on the outside of the envelope in pencil was the name Ruby. Eva remembered the day her mother had asked if she could see baby Ruby.

Oh, so there was a baby Ruby, she said to herself.

Finding out about baby Ruby proved to be difficult as there was no one she could ask. Martha's siblings were all dead and she was not sure how to proceed. There had not been a death certificate for a baby called Ruby amongst her mother's papers—in fact there was no other mention of her anywhere.

Eva went to Queensland with her husband for a few weeks then returned to her position as practice manager at the Greenmount Medical Centre.

41

Dr Sutton

When Eva resumed work at the Medical Centre she was greeted warmly by the staff who were thankful to have her back. There had been two changes to the medical and nursing staff while she was away and she was introduced to them on her first day back during her morning tea break: one very experienced registered nurse who had changed a number of things in the treatment room by ordering various new items which would make work easier for all the medical staff, and a newly qualified general practitioner called Dr Penelope Sutton. Dr Sutton had just moved into the area and mentioned to someone that she did not know anyone except the staff at the Medical Centre as yet. Eva overheard the conversation and later in the day when they had a moment together, she asked her if she would like to come to her place on Saturday afternoon when a few of her friends would be coming for a visit.

"That's kind of you, I would love to come. Should I bring something?" she asked?

"No just come, there will be plenty to eat and drink."

The following Saturday Mandy was the first to arrive at Eva's home.

"I hope all of you won't mind that I have invited someone new from the Medical Centre," Eva told Mandy. "She is a new GP, and also new to the area so she doesn't know anybody yet."

"I certainly don't mind," Mandy said, "and I doubt that the others will; the more the merrier."

Astrid and Marjorie arrived together followed by Felicity and Jane, who was carrying her usual plate of homemade savouries. The doorbell rang and Eva got up to let in the new arrival, Dr Penelope Sutton. Mandy looked up and gasped as she recognised Penny, the doctor she had worked with on that dreadful night years ago. Eva was busy introducing Penny to everyone and was not aware that Mandy had become silent and extremely pale.

"What's wrong Mandy?" asked Astrid, who had noticed. "Are you unwell?"

"No, I've just had a bit of a shock that's all," she replied, staring at the new arrival. Penny by this time had noticed Mandy and she also showed signs of shock and surprise. The room was quiet now as they both stared at each other, not knowing what to say for what seemed like ages. Then Eva took Penny by the hand and sat her down. Mandy stood up and went to the kitchen where she sat at the table, her head in her hands.

Felicity went to Mandy. "What is it, what has happened?"

"Penny is the doctor who was there on the night of that terrible incident that ruined my career, after the child's treatment was mismanaged and she died."

"Oh! So that's it. Is this the first time you have seen her since?"

"Yes. And I was totally unprepared for that eventuality."

Felicity got Mandy a glass of water and sat with her at the table holding her hand. The door to the kitchen swung open and Penny entered and sat down opposite Mandy.

"Mandy, I am as shocked as you are but I am so glad to see you,"

Penny said. "I know we have a lot to talk about. We need to clear the air."

Felicity said she would leave them alone and left the room, closing the door behind her.

The two women stayed closeted in the kitchen for about an hour going over everything they remembered about that night and the subsequent events.

Penny began, "I tried to get in touch with you but I was told you were on leave and I was not able to obtain your phone number. I was also on leave and not in a good frame of mind so eventually I gave up."

"Oh, so you were on leave after that incident too?" asked Mandy, surprised.

"Yes. I was made to feel responsible for the child's death and I had to take time off because of the way I felt," Penny answered "It was awful. The registrar was accused of not supporting me so he threw me under the bus, so to speak, by saying I had not informed him of the child's deteriorating condition. It was not true—we were both very busy that night and every time I contacted him he just kept telling me to stick to the consultant's orders. I don't know if he contacted him or not. When I was interviewed by the consultant he just wouldn't listen to me and when I tried to tell him what I thought had gone wrong, he didn't want to hear what I had to say. I had the feeling I was the only one of the team who cared about the child. I was so badly affected by the whole thing that I had to take some leave. It made me change my career plans completely and I decided to become a GP."

"Oh," said Mandy, "That's more or less what happened to me. I was wretched afterwards because I was also thrown under the bus, and I don't know what affected me more—the little girl dying or the lack of support and caring by my colleagues."

"So really we were both in the same boat," said Penny. "Did you go back to work eventually?"

"No. But I am glad you were able to resume medicine because you are a good doctor. I am much older than you and that, sadly, ended my nursing career."

The two women hugged each other and returned to the other room where the other guests were talking quietly together. Penny and Mandy were given a glass of wine each and some food and some normality returned to the room.

Mandy had been shocked to see Penny but now felt very glad that she had, not because Penny had suffered too but because it had made her feel less alienated.

42

Ruby

Eva became obsessed with trying to solve the riddle of Ruby. She went through everything belonging to her mother again and again but no further information about Ruby surfaced. She got in touch with several cousins who were around her age but none of them knew anything about a baby called Ruby. One night when she couldn't sleep a thought popped into her mind. Her mother had kept in touch with two cousins who lived in New Zealand; it was only an exchange of Christmas cards but she decided to write to them as a last resort. Although Martha had only kept in touch with these two women at Christmas time, Eva knew they had families, but she had never had anything to do with them and did not even know their names. It was not difficult to find the addresses of the families as Martha had kept the same address book for sixty years. Not sure who to address the letters to, she wrote two and sent them to 'The Family of Mrs Pat Taylor' and 'The Family of Mrs Joan Watkins'.

It was a while before she received a reply and the news she received upset her so much she began to sob with sadness and anger and desperation at what the letter revealed about the unfairness that had existed for women and children in the past.

43

Marjorie

Astrid and Julie arrived home after school pick up to find Marjorie almost bursting with excitement.

"Come into the kitchen. I have made a cake to celebrate," she said.

"Celebrate what?" Julie asked, eyeing the chocolate cake.

"Sit down, sit down, and I will tell you all about it, I have just made a pot of tea."

They all sat at the table and Marjorie poured three cups, added milk and began telling them her news.

"I'm so excited: I had a phone call from London today from Angela, and you will never guess what she told me."

"I can't guess," said Astrid. "What did she say?"

"She's having a baby, she's three months pregnant."

"That's wonderful!"

"But that's not all—she and her husband are coming to Australia to live and will be here long before the baby's due. They want the baby to be born and brought up in Australia."

"Will they want to live here, will we have to move?" inquired Julie anxiously, looking from Marjorie to Astrid.

"No, they will be living in Melbourne because of Phillip's work. They might stay with us at first but no Julie, this is your home now and you and Astrid can stay for as long as you want."

Julie breathed a visible sigh of relief.

"A new baby, there is nothing as nice as a new baby in the family," said Astrid.

"Ah but wait, there's more, I have more news." Marjorie took a breath and said, "Bethany and her fiancé are coming to Australia to be married in the summer."

Astrid gave Marjorie a big hug and said, "That is worth celebrating, let's take the children and go to the local pub for dinner, I'll ring Mandy and Jane, they might like to come to."

"Ring Eva and Felicity too, they would probably like a night out."

At the pub Marjorie bought champagne and they toasted the expected baby, Angela and Bethany and numerous other things. The children joined in, clinking their glasses filled with mineral water and cheering excitedly. There was a band playing that night so after dinner the women got up and danced with the children to the live music.

On the way home they all walked arm in arm still singing the songs they had been dancing to.

"We are so lucky to have each other," said Astrid.

"Women need supportive female friends and we have them in spades," Jane replied.

"Between us we have experienced so much and we have survived," Mandy added.

"I hope we can always be as close as we are today," Felicity responded.

44

Martha's Secret

Eva rang Felicity and asked her to come to her house on Saturday.

As soon as Felicity looked at Eva she knew immediately that something was seriously wrong. She put out her arms and drew her into an embrace. "What is it, what's wrong?"

Eva tried not to cry but tears welled up in her eyes and began to fall down her cheeks.

"A few weeks before Mum died she mentioned that she wanted to see a baby called Ruby but I didn't take much notice, I just thought she was imagining things. After she died and I was going through her things, I found an envelope with Ruby written on it and inside was a lock of hair tied with a pink ribbon."

"Oh wow, that is strange I suppose," said Felicity.

"Yes, strange because I had never heard her mention a baby called Ruby."

"Could she have had a baby who died, perhaps?" asked Felicity.

"I did think of that, but there was no death certificate. I asked everyone in the family but no one knew anything. Then I decided to write to some distant relatives of Mum's in New Zealand and I received an amazing answer."

"What? Tell me, what did they tell you?"

"Ruby is still alive and living in New Zealand, her name is Margaret Ruby Thompson. She is married and has four children and several grandchildren."

"So you found her—that's wonderful."

"Yes, and she is my older sister who was born before my parents were married! My father was overseas during the war and my grandparents made her give the baby up for adoption."

Eva began to cry again. "Now I know why my mother was so nervous about me having anything to do with the opposite sex and why she was so scared of me getting pregnant before being married. She had been through a pregnancy, a birth and relinquishing a baby out of wedlock and I suppose she feared the same thing could happen to me."

"Oh Eva, what a shock, but it's a nice shock surely," said Felicity.

"It is..." responded Eva slowly. "I've always wished I had a sister and I do have a sister, but I have only just found out. It's awful."

"What are you planning to do?"

"I am going to New Zealand as soon as I can."

"Let's have a cup of tea," said Felicity.

"No, let's have a glass of wine," Eva said, moving to the fridge.

45

Ruby

Eva didn't go to New Zealand. She didn't have to because Ruby came to Australia almost at once. She had known most of her life that she was adopted but only since the family received Eva's letters had she learnt the truth from an older sister in New Zealand about her adoption. Not wasting time in ringing or writing she just booked a ticket with Air New Zealand and got on a plane heading for Australia. On arrival at Melbourne airport she hired a car with satellite navigation, keyed in Eva's address and headed north. It was not until she pulled into the driveway of Eva's house that she began to feel that perhaps she was being a bit hasty.

Maybe I'd better find somewhere to stay nearby and ring Eva in the morning, Ruby thought as she restarted the car and began to reverse down the driveway. Before she reached the wide gateway the front door opened and a woman with a very familiar face emerged. They stared at each other as Eva slowly moved closer to the car. Simultaneously Ruby opened the car door and stood up on the gravel driveway. Neither of them said a word but they embraced and cried in each other's arms.

46

Mandy

Mandy was finally ready to have her party. Her fracture had healed and she was almost as mobile as before. She hunted out the lists she had made previously and referred to what she had written some time ago and realised she would have to add quite a few more people to the list now and a lot more food to provide for the extra people. A very big, elaborate cake was added to the food list. The drinks would now include champagne as well as red and white wine, non-alcoholic cocktails and mineral water. It was a much bigger venture now but she thought it was going to be well worth the effort.

With so many more things to do she was glad her daughter Poppy was arriving with her husband a week before the party and would stay with them and help with the preparations. Poppy and her husband and children had not been to visit for more than a year and had hinted that they might be returning to live in Melbourne again soon. Mandy had her fingers crossed.

The theme for the party was spring so when Mandy invited people she requested that they wear pink, green or white to her party. She hired a big white marquee and decorated it with pink and green helium balloons tied to the backs of the chairs. Everything else was white, the chairs, the table cloths and the big cake. She bought magic wands and pink and green fairy wings for the children to wear.

Wayne arrived with Grace and the four children. Ruth and Amy along with the other little girls were given pink and green sashes to wear around the waist of their white dresses as well as the fairy wings. With the daughters of Jane, Astrid and Poppy there were six little fairies dancing and twirling beneath the trees in Mandy's garden. The little boys were play fighting using their magic wands as swords until Wayne stepped in and turned them around to become magic wands, but as soon as his back was turned they became swords again. Most people had done what Mandy had asked and wore pink, green and white and it gave the effect of a pretty pastoral scene which was just what she had envisaged.

Standing at the window looking outside Mandy smiled at the sight of her new friends and her family, all people whom she loved, enjoying themselves together in her home. Astrid was sitting with Grace as she breastfed baby Fin who patted his mother's breast with his chubby little hand and stared up at her with absolute adoration. Grace had one arm around Tommy who was leaning into her side, and as she turned and kissed him on the forehead he smiled up at her. Thankfully it looked like Tommy would be alright with his stepmother.

Felicity appeared from around the side of the house wearing a long white shift dress. Her hair was sprayed pink and she had a couple of green feathers dangling from her ears. Her husband Jack followed looking for all the world like a school principal even though he was at a party. He seemed to be grinning at everyone in apology for his wife's eccentric outfit. Little did he know most people loved the way she looked. Eva arrived with her new-found sister Margaret Ruby and they were so alike they could have been twins. At the same time, Jane's parents hurried in looking around at all the unfamiliar faces and Mandy rushed to their side to welcome them.

Marjorie and Granny Peggy were sitting together underneath the rose arbour, probably talking about their shared love of patchwork and quilting. George was standing with his sister Poppy who was dressed in an off-white dress and had a coronet of pink flowers in her hair.

There was music playing but suddenly it stopped and George, who was standing at the top of the stairs, called out to his mother, "Mum, where is Jane?"

"Here she is," said Mandy and as she spoke the familiar tune of 'Here comes the bride' began to play.

Everyone stared at Jane as she emerged from the house in a white lace dress carrying a bunch of pink peonies highlighted with green foliage; she was a beautiful bride.

Everyone was astonished as it had been a well-kept secret, hardly anyone knew except George, Jane, Mandy, John and the marriage celebrant of course. They had even managed to keep it from the children. The couple approached the celebrant and called for all the children to come close and sit on the timber dance floor, then they invited the adults to come and stand behind the children.

Jane and George had written their own wedding vows which they exchanged, causing a few happy tears to fall. The celebrant performed a simple ceremony interspersed with poignant anecdotes told to her by the couple and George's family. It was such a wonderful surprise and everyone was so happy for the couple that they applauded and cheered. The children loved all the cheering and joined in noisily and had to be asked to stop so the ceremony could continue. There were a few speeches and Jane's son William, who was only nine, wanted to say something also. The onlookers smiled broadly and some were moved to tears as William said quietly that he liked George because he made his mummy happy. Jane and George hugged him and his sister Zoe said, "me too, me too."

The following few hours were a lot of fun filled with laughter, happiness, love and goodwill shared between so many people of similar ilk.

Mandy returned to the house to bring out some clean glasses; as she was about to exit the back door there was a knock at the front door then a ringing of the door bell.

'Who can that be?' Mandy muttered to herself. She put the tray of glasses on the hall table and peered through a side window. Standing on the front veranda holding a bunch of flowers was a slim pretty woman. Mandy stared, not recognising her at first, then realised it was Kathy.

'Oh no, what is she doing here? This day of all days; this could cause some problems,' Mandy said under her breath. She stood for a moment thinking about what she should do. Turning quickly she shut the door leading into the living room then returned and opened the front door.

"Hello Kathy, what a surprise to see you." Mandy tried to make her voice sound as normal as possible.

"Yes I haven't seen you for a long time. Mum said I should write you a letter to thank you for all your help but I decided to bring you a bunch of flowers instead."

Mandy couldn't leave her standing outside holding the flowers she had travelled so far to deliver. "Come in for a while," she said.

Fortunately there was a small study just inside the front door.

"Come in and sit here," she said to Kathy. "Would you like a cold drink?"

"Yes please," Kathy replied. "Are you having a party? I can hear music."

"Just a family get-together," lied Mandy. "How did you get here, Kathy?"

"I came on the train. There are trains going back to the city every hour I think so I will go back later. It was a long walk from the station… I would like drink of water."

Mandy sped to the kitchen, being careful to close the door behind her. When she returned with the water Kathy was out of the study and walking towards her. Mandy walked back into the study and Kathy followed her. Placing the glass of water on the desk she asked Kathy to sit and drink.

"How are you Kathy, are you still living with your parents?"

"Yes, I will stay with them until Wayne comes to get me," she answered with a smile.

"Oh I see," Mandy replied, thinking this visit could be a disaster if she sees Wayne and the children outside.

"I know he will come soon," Kathy repeated.

Mandy began to feel quite worried. What the hell am I going to do, she thought. Whatever I do it had better be quick.

"Would you like me to drive you to the station Kathy? Then you will be sure to catch the next train."

"Yes, that would be good, it's a long way to walk."

Fortunately Mandy always kept her car keys on the hall table close to the front door. Picking them up she beckoned to Kathy and hurried her out the front door.

As they backed out of the driveway, Kathy said, "You must have a big family, there are so many cars in the street."

"Yes, there are a lot of cars," agreed Mandy, praying that no one Kathy knew came out of the house. Thankfully no one did, and as Mandy turned the corner she breathed a sigh of relief. She stayed with Kathy until she was safely on the train heading back towards Melbourne. Driving back to the party Mandy felt an enormous amount of shame at what she had just done to Kathy. Under different circumstances she would never have hurried her out of the house and out of sight as she had. That was very cruel and heartless, she thought to herself, but if I had invited her in to the party, who knows what could have happened. Her children in particular would have been traumatised and confused at seeing her so unexpectedly, and goodness knows how she would have reacted to the sight of Wayne with Grace and the children.

Returning home, she saw George and Jane at the front door obviously looking for her.

"Mum, where have you been?" asked George.

"I'm coming, I'll tell you all about it."

Everyone agreed it would have been a disaster if poor Kathy had seen what was going on.

Wayne rang Kathy's parents who had no idea where she was and had been searching for her for the past hour.

"Oh my goodness, I need a strong cup of coffee after that," said Mandy. "Let's get on with the party, it will be time for the bride and groom to leave soon and we haven't even cut the cake."

www.ingramcontent.com/pod-product-compliance
Lightning Source LLC
Chambersburg PA
CBHW070032120726
47909CB00003B/1134